"Elise."

She pointed behind him. Jonah turned but couldn't see what she was trying to show him. Did she even know it was him? A guttural noise emerged from her throat.

"EMTs will be here in a minute." He could hear the ambulance's siren, close enough it was probably turning from Hancock onto the road that led to the zoo.

Her mouth moved, her lips forming a word he didn't understand.

"Elise, I don't know what you're saying." What had happened to her? This woman on the floor was nothing like the vibrant woman he'd known. She was dressed for a safari, but the zoo was a wreck. No one should even be here.

"Elise."

Her face reddened. Her mouth moved again, and she managed to say, "Bomb."

Jonah understood that word. He grabbed up his flashlight and spun to shine it in the direction she'd pointed. Taped to the underside of the grimy desk, it was no bigger than the lockbox for a handgun.

He swiped Elise from the floor, lifting her tiny body easily. He burst from the office door into the night, vaulting the steps.

The building behind them exploded in a boom and a rush of flames.

Lisa Phillips is a British-born, tea-drinking, guitar-playing wife and mom of two. She and her husband lead worship together at their local church. Lisa pens high-stakes stories of mayhem and disaster where you can find made-for-each-other love that always ends in happily-ever-after, and she understands that faith is a work-in-progress more exciting than any story she can dream up. Lisa blogs monthly at teamloveontherun.com, and you can find out more about her books at authorlisaphillips.com.

Books by Lisa Phillips

Love Inspired Suspense

Double Agent
Star Witness
Manhunt
Easy Prey

EASY PREY

LISA PHILLIPS

HARLEQUIN LOVE INSPIRED® SUSPENSE

Recycling programs
for this product may
not exist in your area.

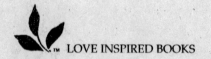 LOVE INSPIRED BOOKS

ISBN-13: 978-0-373-67705-4

Easy Prey

This is my comfort in my affliction,
for Your word has given me life.
—*Psalms* 119:50

To the wild animals that live in my house.
Thanks for making every day messy and smelly and fun.

ONE

First day on the job, first day back in her hometown—and Elise Tanner had no idea what to expect. The evening cast shadows in the corners between the portable buildings that housed the zoo's offices. The treatment and feed centers were now broken-down shells of buildings across the expanse of intersecting concrete pathways from the empty enclosures. The fifty-acre zoo looked menacing even in its disrepair.

Beside her, Elise's seventeen-year-old son, Nathan, switched the flashlight app on his phone and held it up, shining it around the zoo's entrance.

"Nice place." He flicked the hair out of his eyes and looked at her, his gaze wide at the state of the zoo. "I'm gonna go look around."

She smiled, sharing his impression of a facility that might have been impressive before it was completely flooded out. At least, impressive for a tiny zoo in a small town. "Be careful."

He would be, she knew that. Nathan had lived his whole life in a wild animal sanctuary surrounded by tigers, bears and even a manatee. He got along better with creatures than people most of the time, but she couldn't help worrying. Who knew what state the zoo was in beyond the entrance area? Most of the buildings had been condemned.

They probably should have waited until tomorrow to look around, but curiosity had gotten the better of her and it wasn't totally dark. What was the point in sitting around their hotel rooms when they could check the place out? After all, fixing it up was the reason they were here.

Elise climbed the wooden steps to the office. It was late, and they'd been driving most of the day. She felt every one of her forty years tonight.

The stairs swayed, the rickety wood threatening to collapse under her extra fifteen pounds—the ones her best friend said were all in her head. Everything here had been drowned under dirty water that had risen higher than anyone expected. It was no wonder the stairs were almost rotted out.

The infrastructure of the zoo had been woefully outdated even before the water, but the destruction that occurred was beyond imagining.

Trees downed, and fences washed away. Enclosures had been completely ruined. The water quality in the lake didn't bear thinking about, and the zoo's old, blind tiger had gone missing weeks before and had not been seen since. Fortunately the animals had been transported out of town in the initial evacuation.

She was going to have to rebuild this whole place from scratch.

Elise had read all about the flood online, far away from her Oregon hometown in a wild-animal sanctuary she'd been working at in Idaho. It was where she'd gone to escape the pain and grief of losing her husband just weeks into his first deployment. She'd spent years pouring into Nathan and her animals in that safe haven. Now she was home. For as long as this took, at least.

Elise had no illusions. She'd been head-hunted by the mayor because she'd grown up here, and because she was also the only person he knew who was qualified to manage his zoo.

It had taken a lot for Elise to leave her safe haven, but Nathan would be headed to college soon. She had to pay his tuition somehow.

As long as she could manage to not run into anything that reminded her of those long-ago days. At least not before she handed the running of the zoo off to someone else, then she just might survive this with her heart intact.

Maybe.

Inside the office was dark, but she could hear someone moving around. Elise flipped the light switch. Nothing. Not that she'd expected the power to be on, but wishful thinking had to count for something.

Elise pulled the flashlight from the belt of her "animal worker" outfit of dark green cargo pants and a dark green buttoned shirt. There was no sense in getting her regular clothes torn or dirty from the devastation, so she'd worn her work uniform from the Idaho sanctuary.

She flipped the flashlight on and shone the light at the figure. A man. "Who are you?"

The drab-clothed guy turned around. The dead eyes of a stranger stared back at her, making the pale skin of his face even starker. Probably not much older than her, he didn't remove his hands from the filing cabinet drawer where he'd been riffling through papers. They were *her* papers now, in *her* office.

His eyebrow rose. "I think the question is, who are *you*?"

Elise had dealt with trespassers before. But never an overly curious one. They usually only wanted to take a souvenir, or to leave their mark—with vandalism.

Elise set her hands on her hips and tried to look authoritative even though she was barely five-three. She studied his face, trying to remember if she'd met him when she lived here before. She didn't think he was anyone she used to know, and he evidently didn't care she'd seen his face. "I'm in charge of this zoo now. You need to leave the premises before I call the cops."

Tree limbs brushed the window of the portable building. There were two desks and a row of file cabinets, most of which had open drawers. Papers were all over the place, like a gust of wind had blown them into disarray—or this guy had been searching awhile.

His eyes narrowed and he ran at her.

Elise tried to dodge him, but he slammed into her like a football player single-handedly tackling the opposing team's defensive line. Breath whooshed from her lungs as her back hit the wall. The flashlight slipped from her hand to light a strip of carpet on the floor.

Dazed, she realized the man was reaching for her belt. She heard the jangle of keys and felt the pull that meant he was trying to take them from her. The retractable string holding the key ring on her belt was pulled all the way out as the man backed up. With a vicious yank he tore the string from its clasp, taking the zoo keys with it.

Elise reached for her cell phone, but it wasn't in the holder on her belt. It must have fallen out. She looked around, but the floor was in shadows except for the beam of her flashlight.

The man moved. Elise tried to track his steps in the dim light, but couldn't get a fix on him. Dark overcoat. He was taller than her, maybe five-seven. The heavy material gave the illusion of bulk, but he'd had plenty of strength to slam her against the wall.

She moved toward the back door, just a step, praying the route was clear. The man swung at her, something hard colliding with her back. The impact sent her to her knees. Elise scrabbled around on the floor, praying her cell was close by. Nathan didn't need to come here and get hurt, but he could get help. Another hit sent her to the floor so she lay prone, stunned. Pain held her lungs frozen so she couldn't get air.

All she could do was watch as the man went to the same file cabinet he'd been looking in only minutes ago and pulled out a handful of papers. His dirty loafer nearly stomped her hand as he ran past where she lay, out the door.

Elise lay there helpless, waiting for someone

to find her. She glanced around, trying to spot her phone. Her eyes caught on something taped to the underside of the desk. Wires. Blocks of gray stuff that looked like molding clay.

A bomb?

Jonah Rivers keyed the mic on his collar as he ran. "The fugitive is headed into the zoo. I'm in pursuit."

The man he chased had lived on chips and cigarettes for years, while Jonah ate as healthy as any other single deputy US marshal. He also worked out every day but Monday—because Mondays were bad enough without adding having to work out. Jonah headed up the Northwest fugitive apprehension task force, US marshals who hunted the lowest of the low—those who had escaped custody, or hadn't shown up for their court appearances. Fugitives. The most wanted.

Eventually Fix Tanner would slow, and Jonah was going to catch him.

It was what he did.

Too bad Fix Tanner and his little sister had been a steady part of Jonah's youth. Although Fix had always held himself separate from Jonah and his brother—the rich kids. Fix and his sister had grown up in a double-wide with their alcoholic mom.

Now it was just another day, just another fugitive.

A car with out-of-state plates and a sticker in the back window—a rental—was parked outside the entrance. Jonah ran, legs pumping, hands gripping his Glock in front of him. Sweat chilled on his forehead as he jumped over strewn two-by-fours, branches and other debris. The floodwaters had reached roof height, and this place was a mess.

He'd been chasing this guy for two miles already. Had Fix found a place to hunker down?

Jonah didn't know of any connection the man had to the zoo, now or back when it'd been open. The previous manager had been killed in the flood, his body never found. Jonah had heard they were bringing in someone new to reopen it, some kind of wild-animal expert. But he had bigger things to worry about than an attraction he was never going to visit.

"We're coming in the east entrance but there's a lot of debris." Hanning's voice was breathy.

Deputy Marshal Eric Hanning was a member of Jonah's team. He was also engaged to another teammate, Deputy Marshal Hailey Shelder. The two had fallen in love after they were forced to rely on each other during the recent flood, when the team had been hunting an escaped convict.

Jonah had been shot in the stomach, and promoted, all during that same manhunt. Now he was in charge of not just the team but the whole office.

Of course Jonah had wanted the job one day, but not like that—not because their former boss had turned bad. The team hadn't seemed to mind, even though it took a few weeks recovering from his wounds for Jonah to settle in. Boss or not, Jonah would always be a boots-on-the-ground kind of marshal.

The man he was chasing now was low-level. Fix Tanner hadn't shown up for his court appearance, but Jonah wanted him for more than just the fact that he should be in jail. Fix had a boss. Fix's boss had a boss. That made for a lot of fingers in a lot of pies, all of which were here in his town. Jonah wanted charges brought against all of them.

The door was open on the first building, so Jonah stepped silently up the stairs, slowing his pace. Blood rushed in his head, and the beat of his heart pounded in his ears in the silence. If one of his team radioed in now, the sound would be deafening.

While Hanning and Shelder took the east

entrance, his other two team members, Jackson Parker and Wyatt Ames—a former SEAL and a former police detective, respectively—were on the west side. The zoo wasn't all that big. Fifty acres. It should take minutes for them to meet in the center where the lake was.

Jonah flipped on his flashlight and scanned the room.

The beam moved over a body—a woman. Jonah crouched and touched her shoulder. She shifted, moaning as though the soft touch hurt, but it was her warmth that sent a rush of relief through him. He couldn't help her if she was dead, and murder investigations weren't his jurisdiction.

Jonah pulled out his cell phone and called emergency dispatch, then informed his teammates of what he'd found. "Anyone got a location on Tanner?"

"Negative."

"Not yet." Parker's determination was only in part due to his having been a SEAL. The man was also incredibly stubborn.

"Keep searching," Jonah said. "I'll wait with her."

"Her?" The interest in Ames's voice was unmistakable.

"She's hurt, Ames. But it's not Tanner, it's a woman."

Jonah turned his attention to her. Had Fix Tanner done this? He wouldn't put it past the man, but Jonah had been chasing him only minutes ago. Now Fix was who knew where, and this woman had been hurt because Jonah wasn't fast enough.

Was his wound slowing him down? It was down to a dull ache most days, and he didn't want to keep to his desk, but he didn't want to put the team—or anyone else—in jeopardy, either.

He shouldn't turn the woman if she was injured, but he brushed the hair back from her face enough to see who it was.

His voice was a whisper. "Elise."

Flashes of the past ran through his brain like a movie reel. Cookouts, the lake and little Elise Tanner. They'd been friends all the time he was in high school, right up until he joined the marines. And then come home from deployment to find she'd married his brother.

Crumpled in a heap on the floor wasn't just any woman. This happened to be *the* one woman in the world he'd never imagined he would ever see again, and now she was here. Jonah sank to his knees beside her and checked his watch. Emergency services wouldn't be long.

"Elise?" He patted her cheek. It couldn't be

a coincidence she was here on the exact day Jonah was chasing her brother.

The years had changed both of them—that much was obvious. Still, in his heart she was the same smiling, teenage girl. Years lay between today and the day Jonah had returned from yet another deployment to discover she'd left town, consumed with her grief over his brother being killed in action.

For months his heart had warred between acknowledging she was simply grieving and the fact she hadn't wanted him to help her through it. They'd had a close relationship once, but that apparently didn't matter. She hadn't trusted Jonah enough to be there for her when she needed it. She'd just banked the death benefits and left his mom's pool house without so much as a note.

Chasing her down and demanding an explanation—or just making sure she was okay—wouldn't have brought him any kind of satisfaction. She'd probably hated him for talking his brother into a military career. He'd hated himself well enough that Jonah hadn't figured he could handle her anger on top of his guilt.

What was she doing back in town after all these years? He didn't want to believe it had something to do with her brother, Fix, but if it did, then Jonah would have to face the consequences.

"Elise." Jonah didn't want to admit how much it hurt just saying her name. He refused to admit he'd missed her, even to himself.

She sucked in a breath and coughed it out. Her eyes flew open and she gasped, but she wasn't looking at him.

"Elise."

She pointed behind him. Jonah turned, but couldn't see what she was trying to show him. Did she even know who he was? A guttural noise emerged from her throat.

"EMTs will be here in a minute." He could hear the ambulance's siren, close enough it was probably turning from Hancock onto the road that led to the zoo.

Her mouth moved, her lips forming a word he didn't understand.

"Elise, I don't know what you're saying." His stomach churned. What had happened to her? This woman was dressed for a safari, but the zoo was a wreck. No one should even be here.

"Elise."

Her face reddened. Her mouth moved again, and she managed to say, "Bomb."

Jonah understood that word. He grabbed up his flashlight and spun to shine it in the direction she'd pointed. Taped to the underside of the grimy desk, it was no bigger than the lock-box for a handgun.

He swiped Elise from the floor, lifting her body easily the way he'd done plenty of times in his mom's pool. He burst from the office door into the night, vaulting the steps.

The building behind them exploded in a *boom* and a rush of flames.

TWO

The man dived and rolled, taking Elise with him. Aside from the bomb—which to be fair, was a pretty major distraction—she just couldn't think of this man as being her Jonah. He didn't look like Jonah, he didn't sound like Jonah and he certainly didn't smell like Jonah. Elise had spent years with animals and a boy, and Jonah didn't smell like anything she recognized. He smelled…like a man.

Tucked against him, she could only hold on as they turned over and over against the ground. Pain stabbed across her back and she yelled, even as she felt the heat of the flames on her face. Smoke choked the clean air from her lungs. The night sky flashed orange and they came to a stop.

Emergency sirens filled the air and people yelled. Boots pounded the ground to where they lay. Elise lifted her chin until she could see Jonah's face. He didn't say anything. He just stared down at her, a mix of disbelief and some of the warmth she remembered.

"Hi, Jonah."

The warmth dissipated. "Now you're going to acknowledge me?"

It was like being doused with ice water. "There was a bomb." Hadn't that been more important than their reunion? It'd been more important than the pain on her back.

Elise pushed away from him. She'd thought they were having a moment, but apparently not. The movement took her breath away.

He got up. "Are you okay?"

She shut her eyes and lay back, sucking air through her nose. How hard had that guy hit her? The world rotated and she put her hand to her forehead. She didn't want Jonah feeling sorry for her out of guilt, but he already knew she was hurt. What was the point in pretending?

"What happened, Elise? Why were you on the floor? What are you even doing here?"

Elise opened her eyes. "Someone in the office. Hit in the back. Job."

He frowned. "You're the new zookeeper?"

Two EMTs ran up, setting bulky bags beside her. Elise tried to answer their questions. It was hard to find a single thought, let alone string two together. All the while Jonah stood there.

People walked up and spoke to him, uniformed cops and stern-faced men—and one woman—with silver star-shaped badges on their hips.

Jonah nodded to them. "Yes. Get on that."

The badge people all strode off.

From the look of things, Jonah was someone important. His blond hair was still military short, highlighting his high-set cheekbones and steel-gray eyes. That much remained of the guy she'd known, his features so much like his brother's. The same features bequeathed to her son, so that she'd had to see them every single day of Nathan's life, forced to remember everything she'd lost.

Jonah's T-shirt was overlaid with a black bulletproof vest. The gun on his hip and the badge on his belt only solidified the air of authority he'd always carried. Even in high school, years before he joined the marines, he'd been that way.

She lifted her eyes to his face, to where the man who had once been her best friend, her husband's brother, now stared angrily down at her.

Nathan's uncle.

Why had she thought she could escape the reckoning that was only inevitable when Jonah found out he had a nephew? Maybe it was the real reason she was here—more than just Nathan's college tuition. Her son did need to know his relatives.

Or Jonah, at least. His mom—Nathan's grandma—was a different story. As was Elise's mom, and her brother.

Jonah shook his head. "What on earth is going on, Elise? I was chasing Fix—"

"My brother?"

Jonah sighed. "He ran into the zoo and disappeared, and then I found you on the floor." He swiped his hands down his face.

Fix had always been wild. Quick to break any rule imposed upon him. But he'd still been her brother, and being estranged from both him and her mother all these years didn't stop Elise from feeling the pang of grief knowing he was a criminal.

Fix had to be in big trouble if cops were after him.

If it wasn't for the influence of the Rivers brothers—Jonah and his brother, her husband, Martin—Elise might very well have ended up walking the same path as Fix.

But for the grace of God.

Every single part of her past had intruded today. She half expected Jonah's mother to walk in the zoo any moment now, just so she could look disapprovingly at Elise one more time.

Elise shook off the bizarre thought and said, "There was a man in the office, but it wasn't Fix. He stole my keys and some files." It made no sense. "The gate doesn't even lock, and he took my keys."

Jonah crouched beside her. "Did the man you saw plant this bomb?"

The EMT jerked, as though hearing the word spoken aloud was entirely different from witnessing an explosion.

"If he did, it was before he searched the place." She waited a moment for her brain to catch up. "I'm surprised there was even anything in the office to find, given how much of a mess this place is in. Nathan went…" The breath left her lungs in a rush.

Jonah frowned. He looked like he was waiting for her to finish.

Elise looked around. Where was Nathan? He must have seen the explosion. And there were cops everywhere.

A man called out, "Hey, Jonah. I think your radio is busted. We found this kid hanging around."

Elise craned her neck to look while Jonah strode toward two marshals walking Nathan between them. Her son's hands were pulled behind his back.

She grabbed the EMT's arm. "Help me up."

He looked at her like she was crazy, but Elise ignored it as she pulled on his shoulder. He raised her to her feet. Trying not to breathe so much that it hurt, she strode over to the marshals holding her son. "Let him go."

"Elise—" Jonah held out a hand, halting her when she would have gone to Nathan. "Stay out of this. Unless you're going to tell me it has something to do with your brother."

Eyes on Jonah, Elise pointed a finger at her son, showing Jonah the stern *mom* face that made Nathan listen even when he didn't want to clean his room. "You let him go."

Jonah said, "Elise—"

"Mom, they think I planted a bomb." Her son's voice wavered.

Jonah's eyes flashed wide. "Mom?"

Who else did Jonah think the kid belonged to? It shouldn't have been that much of a stretch. They both had the same build, the same steel-gray eyes.

"Nathan and I don't have anything to do with your search for my brother." There was no way she would let this new cop version of Jonah tie them up in his business. "We arrived in town this morning. The fact we're here tonight is only a coincidence. We have nothing to do with my brother, or what happened here. Let. Him. Go."

* * *

Jonah looked from Elise, to the teen and back. Steeling himself for the answer, he said, "Is this your son?"

She nodded.

"Is he my nephew?"

The team as a whole shifted in reaction to his question, though Jonah didn't think anyone but someone who worked with them day in and day out would have noticed their reaction.

No one moved. Surrounded by his coworkers, cops and emergency services personnel he knew and who knew him, Jonah waited for Elise to finally tell him the whole truth.

It seemed like an eternity of agony before Elise said, "Yes."

Tears filled her eyes. Jonah couldn't believe what he was hearing. He had a nephew he hadn't even known about? First, Elise had walked out days after Martin's funeral—before Jonah had even managed to get home. Now he was finding out she'd been pregnant?

Why hadn't she ever bothered to tell him she'd had Martin's baby? Never told his mom she was a grandma?

Fury burned inside him. She must have seen it, because she winced.

"Elise—"

"No! Don't you dare blame this on me,

Jonah." She looked at him as though he was
little more than a stranger. Evidently whatever
familiarity they'd had years ago was gone now.

The dark green button-down shirt had a
wild-animal sanctuary logo on it and matched
her green pants, held up by a corduroy belt with
empty holders and a broken key chain. She certainly wasn't a kid anymore. But just like back
then, his heart caught at the sight of her.

Why did he suddenly want to sit her down
and ask her how she'd been?

To cover the slip, he turned to Hanning and
Shelder. Eric looked like a male model, while
Hailey had wild red hair and was a cute tom-
boy. The lovebirds made an interesting pair.
They were also very good at what they did.

"Let the kid go."

The young man passed Jonah, looking up
at him with his brother Martin's silver eyes.
Elise had always called them steel gray, but
Martin's had possessed a light that Jonah had
never seen anywhere else. Until this kid—almost a man, really.

He had Jonah's lanky body—except that it
was actually Martin's, not his. He shouldn't
forget that. Still, the long arms and legs were
familiar enough that he knew Nathan had trouble finding clothes that fit his limbs. Length
might've helped on a basketball court, but

Jonah had found it also meant he had trouble with coordination the rest of the time.

Nathan's hair was styled to sweep across his forehead and fall over his eyes. Jonah was just old enough to find the fact that his nephew probably used styling product in his hair mildly hilarious.

The kid shot him a slightly curious, dirty look, and walked to his mom.

Jonah focused on his team. "Get Parker and Ames. I want the whole zoo searched. We need to find Fix, but keep an eye out for the man who attacked Elise. I'll get you a description."

His female teammate smirked, tipping her head to one side. "Elise?"

Jonah sighed. "Elise Tanner, this is Deputy Marshal Hailey Shelder, who was just leaving, and her fiancé, Deputy Marshal Eric Hanning, who is going with her."

Hailey rushed past him. Jonah turned just in time to see her shake hands with Elise. Hailey practically bounced up and down on her boots. "It's so nice to meet you."

Jonah rolled his eyes, his gaze landing on Eric. He shrugged as if asking, *What are you going to do?*

Jonah knew exactly what. "Shelder. Don't you have a search to do?"

Hailey snapped her boots together and

saluted. "Yes, boss." Eric laughed and the two of them strode away to do something other than nose into Jonah's personal life.

His gaze strayed to Elise. "You'll need to give a statement. Whatever you can tell the police about the man who attacked you is going to help us."

He believed her when she'd said she didn't know the man who attacked her, but her brother could just as easily have been the one who planted the bomb—a pretty good distraction for the marshals chasing him, if he'd had the time to plan it out. Elise could be just another statistic of the victims hurt by Fix Tanner's actions.

Too bad it had to be her.

Why had she come back? The thought that she could be in on Fix's scheme entered his mind, but Jonah dismissed it almost immediately. He was paid to consider all the variables, but he knew Elise wouldn't lie to him. There was just no way.

Except he didn't really know her anymore, did he? Even if they'd been friends for years before he'd come home to his brother's grave and Elise gone. The teenage kid in front of him proved how long it had been. Could he trust her now?

"You said you're here looking for Fix?"

Jonah shifted and showed her where it said US MARSHALS on the back of his vest. "You're in the middle of a manhunt, Lise." She stiffened, but she needed to know the truth of who Fix Tanner was now. "Do you know where your brother is?"

"I haven't seen my brother in…" She faltered. "As long as it's been since I've seen you. I'm telling the truth. We only arrived in town today."

The kid glanced between them. "Mom?"

Elise sighed. "Fix Tanner is my brother. Your uncle."

"And this guy?" The kid motioned to Jonah.

He folded his arms across his chest. "I'm the one who's going to bring Fix Tanner in for his scheduled court appearance."

It was Elise's turn to sigh. "Nathan, this is your other uncle. Your father's brother, Jonah."

Jonah blinked. "His name is Nathan?"

Elise glanced at him like he was an irritant. "You know I loved your father, too. There wasn't much else I could give him, so I named his grandson after him."

He couldn't breathe. He only blinked, trying to comprehend her naming her son after his paternal grandfather. His dad had adored little Elise, and she'd felt the same way. There'd never been a steady father figure in her life.

And now there wasn't one in Nathan's—unless Jonah could change that.

The teenager shook his head. "I don't… I don't even know what I'm supposed to say."

"You don't have to say anything, honey."

Jonah nodded, thinking the same thing. "It's not a big deal, kid." There was time enough for them to process this and everything else that had happened tonight.

Elise spun to him, a look of horror on her face.

Jonah shrugged, but that only made it worse. He and Nathan could talk later. Now was not the time, when the police were waiting to take Elise and Nathan's statements about the intruder and the bomb, and Jonah had to get back to the hunt for Fix. What did she think he'd meant?

Elise shifted. She groaned as if she was in pain. Nathan caught her, which made her cry out louder. He looked at Jonah, fear on his face. Jonah was already there, supporting Elise as they lowered her to the cracked concrete.

"I'm okay. I just couldn't catch my breath."

"You need to get checked out at the hospital." The EMT's face was somber. "I think you might have done serious damage to your back." The guy already had her arm in a tight pressure cuff, not wasting any time. She pulled at the tab to detach its hold on her bicep.

Jonah crouched and stilled her fingers, refusing to register how cold she was. Probably shock. Did he have a blanket in his truck? The EMT produced one before he could even think it through.

"Go with them. We need to know what happened if we're going to find your brother. I'll let my team know what's going on and meet you there."

Elise tried to sit up. "What?"

Jonah stood. "I'm coming to the hospital. Until I figure out what just happened, you don't go anywhere without a police escort."

THREE

"There's no sign of Fix Tanner. We searched the grounds and the outlying streets. He's gone."

Jonah nodded at Hailey Shelder. "If the cops don't need help with the bomb investigation, then head home. We can meet first thing tomorrow and regroup, find out if all of this is related, or just coincidental timing."

The others walked up. Jonah stood in a circle with his teammates: Hailey's fiancé, Eric, the SEAL, Parker, and the former cop, Ames. "I'll see you all back at the office. Seven a.m."

Hopefully he would be able to find an off-duty cop to help keep an eye on Elise. He didn't think she was being targeted per se, but she'd been attacked and a bomb had gone off. Whether the things were related or not, they still had one common denominator—the zoo she was now in charge of. Jonah wasn't willing to risk losing her all over again.

Shelder's lips twitched. "And Elise?"

Ames shot her a look. "You're such a girl."

She folded her arms. "So what if I am?"

Jonah sighed. "One of these days I'm going to fire both of you. I'm the boss now. I can do that."

If he didn't get it over with now, they were going to keep hounding him for details.

"Elise married my brother, Martin. He passed away eighteen years ago, when he was in the army and I was with the marines. I wasn't there with him, I was on a different mission when I found out he'd been killed. By the time I got home, Elise was gone. My mother told me she banked the death benefits and took off."

Parker clapped a hand on his shoulder. "Women."

Shelder gasped. "She was grieving."

"Doesn't matter," Parker said. His eyes were hard, filled with the shadows of the past. "She still lied by not saying anything about having a baby. That boy is Jonah's nephew and he didn't even know the kid existed."

"But—"

"Enough." Jonah shook his head. "Don't worry about it. I'll sort things out with Elise, but it's not going to be resolved tonight. You guys just worry about Fix Tanner."

"Is he really Elise's brother?" Eric asked.

Jonah nodded.

"She's involved, then," Parker said.

"Unlikely, but I'm not going to rule it out."

Parker nodded. "That's good. Stick close to her, and eventually you'll discover what she's lying about."

Jonah frowned.

Shelder shook her head at Parker. "When did you get to be so cynical?"

Jonah wasn't going to hang around for them to argue some more. "I'll see you all in the morning."

He drove his truck to the hospital where they'd taken Elise. It was hard to decide if he was more interested in seeing her or in getting to know his nephew better.

Nathan.

The boy's name brought forth the memory of his own father's warm smile. But then, he supposed that was the point of Elise naming her son after his father. Nathan Rivers, Jonah's dad, had always had a soft spot for the girl from the trailer park across town.

The first day they'd met Elise, she had been a spindly twelve-year-old on the lakeshore. Her older brother, Fix, was supposed to have been watching her. She'd wandered a mile around the lake's beach, looking for turtles, before she met up with Jonah, Martin and their father, who had been fishing.

The minute he saw that gap-toothed smile on the girl with the stringy blond hair and she started talking about the symptoms of shell disease in western pond turtles, Jonah had been thoroughly charmed. His dad, too. The old man had suffered a soft spot for little Elise Tanner that was a mile wide and twice as high. But Martin was the one who'd married her.

Now Elise was a stranger, Jonah had a nephew he'd never met and her brother was number one on his list of fugitives to hunt down and drag back in to custody. Never mind figuring out who had hurt her, lifted her keys and stolen files from the zoo office.

Nathan was in the hall. "Hey."

"How's your mom?"

"They're taking X-rays."

Jonah nodded, unsure what else to do—or say. They weren't at the point he could squeeze the kid's shoulder. Nathan was a stranger, despite the resemblance.

Nathan bit his lip. "Were you in Operation Desert Strike just like my dad?" He must have seen the surprise on Jonah's face, because he said, "I looked it up online. I know all about Iraq back then."

Jonah said, "I wasn't in the same part of the country as Martin." He pushed out a breath, unwilling to think about the gravestone and the empty pool house. Both of them, gone. "I thought your mom left because she didn't want to know me anymore, or be reminded of your dad."

After Elise had gone, there hadn't been much else that made sense. What faith he'd had in a God of love and goodness had died with Martin's death and Elise's leaving.

Why hadn't he tried harder to find her? Maybe he shouldn't have given her up so easily. Their lives hadn't been perfect, but maybe their friendship had been worth fighting for. The fact that he'd loved her was irrelevant now—she'd made her choice.

Now she was back, and his father would've said God brought them here for a reason, which only made him ache for his dad all over again. Jonah didn't want to know about a God who orchestrated life like that. He was the one in charge of his own path.

The old man had passed away before Jonah joined the marines. He'd never gotten to see Jonah become a marshal. Never had to live through Martin's death. Never met his grandson.

Despite everything Jonah could wish to have been different, they were both there now.

He pushed aside the awkwardness and set a

hand on his nephew's shoulder. "I'm glad you're here now."

For whatever reason, Jonah would accept the gift he'd been given for exactly that—a gift. It was what his dad would've wanted.

Nathan's cheeks filled and he pushed out a breath in the same way Jonah had done. "This is super weird."

A smile stretched Jonah's mouth. "It won't be for long, I hope." He let his hand drop. "Did you talk with the police?"

Nathan nodded. "They took my statement. But I was across the zoo and I didn't see anyone. I didn't even know that someone hurt my mom. I just saw the fire, and when I came running those marshals handcuffed me. But it's all good."

Of course it was. Jonah studied the kid, trying to figure out if looking jazzed was his normal state, or a consequence of the night they'd had.

Jonah said, "I'm glad you're good."

Still, he had a feeling things were going to get worse before he figured out what was going on.

Elise sat up on the hospital bed, the bandages tight around her torso. She wasn't hurt too badly, just bruised ribs. Not cracked. But the doctor had told her to take it easy and give her ribs the time they needed to heal.

Elise pressed a hand to her forehead. Nothing that'd happened tonight made any sense. A bomb, and a man stealing papers? Taking her keys? Her brother on the run from the US Marshals?

It was like a sick animal with multiple symptoms that didn't correspond to any one thing. She'd sat up many nights worrying over her furry friends. The worst times were when she had to suffer the helplessness of not being able to fix what was wrong with them.

The door cracked open. Assuming it was Nathan, Elise looked up and smiled. Jonah stopped, still gripping the door handle. His eyes widened and he gave her a tentative smile in return.

Elise rolled her eyes. "What do you want now?"

It was like junior high all over again. Waiting outside for him to give her and Martin a ride home, watching all the cool girls make moony eyes over him. The next day had always been the worst, when she had to deal with their questions and snide comments.

Martin had been in her class, and they'd laughed together over all the attention Jonah got. Martin started to catch the eye of the female population at school after Jonah had graduated, and then things got worse. Still, he'd always said he only had eyes for her.

"I want you to catch me up on everything that happened before the bomb."

Elise frowned at his serious face. "I was attacked. The police have already been in here, asking me a million questions about it. They want me to go to the police station tomorrow and look at mug shots."

Now her brain hurt from answering questions, and she was more tired than the time in Idaho when the snow leopard that was in labor had gone into distress. "I have no more answers. I don't know who took the files and attacked me, and I don't know where Fix is."

When she looked at him, she saw Jonah's face had softened. He set a hand on her shoulder. "Take it easy."

Seriously? "Where's Nathan?"

"I'm right here."

Elise looked at the door. She hadn't even noticed him standing there. She held out her hand and Nathan strode over to sit beside her on the bed. Apparently it took her getting seriously hurt before the teenager would willingly show her affection in public. Go figure.

She gave him her most stern face. "Are you okay?"

He nodded. "Yeah, Mom."

She looked at Jonah. His gray eyes were black despite the fluorescent lights, glaring at her with frustration and anger. "You had a baby and you didn't think to tell me?"

If she'd been standing, she'd have slammed her hands on her hips. "Like you'd even have cared. You left for the marines and never looked back. Not once. Don't lie to me, Jonah. After Martin died you didn't even want to know."

Nathan sighed. "Are you two really going to argue?"

Elise looked back at Jonah in time to see his jaw flex. He said, "Where's your brother, Elise?"

Eighteen years and that was all he had to say to her? "I haven't seen Fix since before I left town." Right after she'd buried her husband, when the best friend she'd needed hadn't even come home. Emotion stuck like a hair ball in her throat.

She said, "You wouldn't even be here if you hadn't disliked Fix from the moment you met him. My brother never did anything but try and impress you and Martin, and you turned your back on all of us. Well, guess what? Apparently you were right about Fix. Congratulations." Elise poured all of her emotion into that last word.

"This has nothing to do with me. Fix made his own choices."

"You're right about that. You only think you have that much power over people. But guess what? We weren't all put on this planet to sit around and wait for you to tell us what we can and can't do. We made our own lives just fine without you."

Elise closed her mouth. The simple fact he was standing in front of her now made her brain twirl like a spinning top, merging losing Martin with Jonah's…desertion. That had sure been what it felt like. Why did he have to come to the hospital? She'd learned not to need him in her life.

Jonah was looking down at her with a dark expression. He'd never worn that face before, not directed at her. Jonah had always had a serious side that meant he never failed to do what was right. It had been hard to coax a smile, or even laughter, out of him—something that hadn't happened too often, even in all the years they'd known each other.

Martin had been much more lighthearted. The partyer, always chasing a laugh. Their relationship had been nothing but fun, until Elise lost both of them.

This Jonah was entirely new. The disappointment on his face had formerly been reserved for his mother's disapproval of Elise's friendship with the Rivers boys. Elise had never before been the recipient of it from him. He had better not look that way at Nathan.

Jonah studied her. "You've changed."

She clenched her jaw, not willing to dignify that with a response. Elise wasn't a perky twentysomething anymore. She dressed like what she was—the single forty-year-old mother of a teenager, who also happened to have a hard-earned doctorate in zoology. Her best friend was always talking about makeovers, but who had time for that?

Jonah, however, looked as though he never missed a workout. His T-shirt was tight on his biceps, and the rest of him just looked...incredibly strong. As though life had forced him to weather the years, always leaning in to the wind, trying to control the direction of it with sheer willpower. Had Martin's death done that?

It was plain to see nothing about her impressed him at all. And why would it? It wasn't like she'd spent seventeen years trying to catch a new man. She'd been way too busy with work and Nathan.

She said, "I'm not the only one who's changed."

"Regardless, I'm going to make sure you and Nathan are safe until we find the guy who hurt you tonight."

"What about Fix?"

"If you say you haven't seen your brother, I believe you. But if you hear from him, I need to know. I am going to catch him. I know he's family, but he's hurt people since you've been gone, Elise." Jonah paused. "Why haven't you talked to him?"

Elise looked aside. She'd known she was going to have to explain it sometime. It might as well be now.

"With you and Martin gone it was like Fix lost all the restraint he'd had. Before I left, things were…bad. Cops coming around, asking if I knew where he was." She bit her lip and looked at Jonah. "When I was told Martin died, I called Fix. He never picked up. I left."

"I'm sorry." Jonah's voice was quiet.

"Can I at least talk to him after you bring him in? I'd like to say something to my brother before I lose the chance."

Jonah stayed silent for a moment. Then he said, "You have my word."

After his pronouncement, Elise didn't figure there was much else worth arguing about. At least not when it was so late, and they'd had such a long day. Tomorrow they would figure out where to go from here. Tomorrow she would look at mug shots and help the police find the bomber. Right now she was so exhausted she just wanted to crawl into bed, pull the blanket over her head and forget she'd ever thought coming back here was a good idea.

But for the one lingering thing she still needed to do—the one thing that would give her the closure to move on with her life— maybe she never would have come back. She'd have found another way to pay for Nathan's college, or help him do it.

But for the fact that one of these days she needed to finally go visit Martin's grave.

In the backseat of Jonah's truck, Elise could barely make out the whispered conversation going on between him and Nathan, who sat up front. Did she want to know what they were talking about?

Elise tried to rouse herself enough to lean forward and listen, but her eyelids were drooping fast. The doctor had given her some good pain medication, the kind that knocked her out.

Jonah hit the brakes, and she flung her hand out to brace against the back of Nathan's seat. "Please tell me that's not your room."

The door to Elise's motel room was wide-open. Even from feet away, inside the car, she could see that her stuff had been deposited everywhere around the room.

Someone had broken in.

FOUR

"You can't stay here."

Why did Jonah feel the need to state the obvious? Elise turned to glare at him. "Where do you expect us to go?"

There was no way she was about to take Nathan to her mom's trailer, the one she'd grown up in. She'd have to find another cheap motel, preferably on the opposite side of town.

Once again they were surrounded by police officers, only this time she'd had to write them an embarrassing list of everything that had been stolen from her ransacked room. A list that included her laptop.

Thankfully Nathan's room, which was next door, hadn't been touched. It was a small comfort that he wasn't being targeted.

"Why don't you come to my house?" Jonah looked startled, as though he hadn't expected to say that.

"There's no way I'm setting one foot in that

mansion." Not when it held only memories of Martin, and his father. "No way." And she wasn't being relegated to the pool house again, either. Even if it did mean she wouldn't have to face his mother.

Nathan's eyebrow rose under the fall of hair on his forehead. Why was he surprised? She'd told him all about Martin growing up rich, and she'd tried to be nice when she told him about Martin's mother.

"Not my mom's house." Jonah's face morphed into a look she wasn't familiar with. "My house."

Elise opened her mouth, and her son put his hand over it. Nathan turned to face Jonah. "We would really appreciate staying with you. Thank you."

She glared at her son, the traitor, while Jonah struggled to keep in a smile. Elise said, "Fine. If I'm going to be railroaded anyway, what's the point in arguing?" She should have known Nathan would side with his uncle.

She shouldn't even be around Jonah—that wasn't what she was here for. And it wasn't going to do her any good to dredge up long-buried feelings. Now they were going to stay at his house? If she wasn't hurt and tired, she would probably argue more.

Elise folded her arms in a huff, which lost its

impact since she had to be gentle with her ribs. "I'm going to need a toothbrush."

Jonah's mouth curled into a smile. "Is it wrong that I think you're cute when you're mad?"

"I'm not mad, I'm exhausted."

Nathan shook his head, mouthing something to Jonah that made him laugh. Elise turned and climbed into the backseat of the car. She tried to stay awake as they drove. There was plenty to occupy her mind, but the interior was warm and the seat cushion gave enough that she slid down. It wasn't long before she gave up the fight.

Elise woke in a bed. The room was small, only the bed and a dresser. On the dresser was a vase of flowers that were too perky to be real, as though someone had tried to make the room appear homey but that was all the effort they'd put into it. Like for a guest room. She rubbed sleep from her eyes and glanced around, but her attention wasn't on the bare walls, or the denim-colored curtains.

Was she really in Jonah's house?

Then again she'd survived an attack, a bomb and a break-in, the day before. Why should she be surprised at the fact that she was in Jonah's home now?

She lifted her arms and caught herself before she stretched. The pain medication she'd taken the night before had waned. She'd have to take more soon. As if on cue, her stomach rumbled. She looked at the clock on the wall. It was past ten? No wonder she was hungry.

Elise found a change of clothes on the end of the bed—shorts and a NAVY T-shirt that were clearly Jonah's, since she had no stuff of her own. How long would it be before the police released the belongings that hadn't been stolen back to her?

The coffeepot in the kitchen was half-full and still hot, so she rummaged in Jonah's cabinets and found a mug. He still took half-and-half in his java, so she added some of that for a treat, along with her usual splash of milk and enough sugar that she'd have some extra energy.

Where were they?

Elise looked out the window, but all she saw was grass and a barn. Jonah, who'd grown up in a mansion on the rich side of town, now had a weathered ranch that strangely fit his personality perfectly—even if it did seem a little forlorn.

Nails clicked on the tile floor, and a tan dog with a black saddle and folded-over ears above a German shepherd's face wandered in, headed for a food bowl.

Jonah had always loved German Shepherds, but this one was mixed with a Collie, which softened the dog's features in a way that was immensely cute.

She smiled at him. "Hello."

The dog eyed her but started eating. Probably worried she would try and take his food. Elise crouched and let the animal get to know her scent. She ran her fingers through his scruff. He was well fed, but lean. They probably ran together.

Years ago she, Jonah and Martin had run together. The idea Jonah now ran with someone who wasn't her—even if it was a dog—weighed on her so suddenly she sat down on the cold tile. Logically he'd have run with other people over the years. After all, it had been close to two decades. Why did it bother her so much now?

Martin was gone, and Jonah was the one still here. He probably hurt over his brother's death as much as she did. Would she ever reach the point when she stopped remembering exactly what she'd lost? Martin. Jonah. Their father. The mess she'd made of all of it was immense. Overwhelmed by the tide of grief and guilt, Elise turned her attention again to the dog.

"Let me guess… Hound?"

The dog's ears pricked up. He closed the gap between them and nuzzled her until her hand cramped from stroking him. Elise lifted the tag on his collar. *Sam.* She chuckled. Jonah had always given his pets normal names like Steve or Wilson.

This was what she needed, some animal therapy. No matter how much she helped an animal, it always seemed to heal something in her at the same time. Animals were a solace she found nowhere else, especially when the grief of losing the Rivers brothers swallowed her. The peace and comfort she got from being around animals—and through sharing that with her son—was a gift from God.

Jonah had probably brought them there knowing Elise would be a sucker for his terminally cute dog. Was he trying to win them over with his animal? Too bad it was sort of working.

"Where's your master, huh?" Of course, the dog didn't actually answer. But there was no one else here to talk to.

The couch looked like someone had slept there. It was like her son to bed down anywhere. He'd slept in animal enclosures many times when they were sick, or when one of the females was giving birth. Nathan was almost a nomad in his sleeping habits, bonding only with her and the animals. He seemed to find home in living beings, and not in a place to return to at the end of the day.

Elise walked to the front door so she could look around outside. The dog padded after her and she stopped at the door. "You want to come?"

Sam looked at her, the fuzzy hair around his muzzle making him look almost like he had a mane. The dog cocked his head and Elise smiled. Should she have expected his company?

Elise pulled a heavy jacket from a hook by the door. "Very well, then." She chuckled. "After you."

"This is so cool." The kid's eyes lit.

Jonah's face stretched in a smile at the excitement on Nathan's face. The old Triumph motorcycle he was restoring sat between them in the dusty barn. In one corner was his own father's old sixties Chevelle, and the horse stalls were piled up with rusty car parts.

When Nathan motioned to it, Jonah immediately knew what he wanted. "Go for it."

Nathan touched the handles reverently. He swung his leg over and sat, grinning like it was Christmas.

Jonah had gone into the office at seven for the meeting about Fix Tanner, and he was wiped. By tonight he was going to be dead on his feet. He'd have to go to bed early like an old man.

Nathan squeezed the handle. If he was younger, he'd probably have been making vroom noises. It hit Jonah then. The hair, the eyes with Martin's light in them. Jonah touched a hand to his chest where the ache of loss over his brother's death had never really gone away.

Eighteen years since he'd been gone, and here was Martin's son, sitting on the bike they had bought together. The bike they had planned to fix up together when Jonah got out of the marines.

Tears filled his eyes. He'd only been thinking about trying to show his nephew the things that were important to him. They needed to base their relationship on something other than the connection they had through Elise. To find a common ground on their own. But all he'd discovered instead was the link they had through his brother.

Jonah and Nathan were inexorably connected. Whether they'd met each other before yesterday or not, their lives were intertwined. And while he'd expected to feel yet more sadness at all he'd lost through not knowing

Nathan as he grew up, Jonah realized he had always possessed something. Even if he never knew it. Nathan had been a part of his life always. A fact that made the long years since Martin's death—the years when he hadn't been able to find Elise—feel a little less like a yawning chasm of loneliness.

Jonah brushed away the heaviness and set his hand on his nephew's shoulder. "Your dad loved this bike the minute he saw it."

Nathan looked up then, a world of hope in his eyes. "Really?"

Jonah nodded. "Martin and I planned to work on it together." He paused then, wondering if the kid was feeling one iota of what he was. Maybe the kid didn't think this was a big deal, but something nagged at him to believe otherwise. To trust. "Maybe, if you want, you could help me work on it."

The light in Nathan's eyes spread to his whole face. "I—" His voice cracked with emotion and he cleared his throat. "That would be cool."

Jonah squeezed Nathan's shoulder. "Great."

Elise backed up from the barn door. This whole experience was a bizarre mesh of not wanting to let go of her son just yet and being ecstatic that Nathan was bonding with his uncle because she loved him and wanted good things for him. It was like being pulled in two different directions, but one thing was clear. If Jonah hurt Nathan he'd see how fast she could go "mama bear."

The dog sat patiently beside her. Elise looked out over Jonah's land. She could see the neighboring ranch, and the drive that stretched out at least half a mile to the road. A car pulled up by the mailbox and deposited a newspaper in the holder below Jonah's mailbox before it drove off, disappearing between the trees.

Elise wrapped Jonah's coat tighter around her. She didn't want to face the awkwardness of having to produce small talk with a man who was essentially a stranger.

She clicked her fingers and the dog fell into step beside her. Elise soaked in the brisk morning air as she walked the drive, reveling in the stretching of her muscles. The world was quiet but for the brush of wind on branches and the distant sounds of traffic. The valley where the town was located sat to the north, down a tall hill.

What had made Jonah want to live so removed from everything? She could understand not wanting work to intrude on his personal life. He probably wanted to keep his home life separate from the fugitives he was chasing—one of whom was her own brother.

If she had her phone she'd try and call Fix, but she had no idea what her brother's phone number was now. Even if she did, it'd been on the floor in the office when Jonah carried her out and the building exploded. Too bad she couldn't even afford another one. Not when her salary would go toward their basic expenses and every extra dollar matched Nathan's car savings. She'd have to see if she could get an inexpensive replacement phone online.

Elise pulled out the newspaper and unrolled it. The headline read Local Source Uncovers Exotic Animal Trade.

Under the bold type was Elise's picture. Her breath caught in her throat at the image that had been posted online by the sanctuary she'd worked for previously. It was from their annual fund-raiser, and she was dressed up with her hair fixed in a complicated updo so tight it had made her head ache all night. They'd given her a commendation that day for all her work with a pair of tiger cubs found when the ATF raided a compound of activists and impounded their stockpile of weapons.

Elise scanned the article—all about the explosion that had further destroyed the zoo. The reporter knew all about her having been hired back to rebuild. But imbedded in the lines of text was the implication the zoo had previously had ties to local exotic animal trading.

The reporter even claimed to have evidence directly linking the zoo to local traders.

It was the last thing they needed. Now the reopening, and Elise's position, would be marred by these accusations. Couldn't he have just stuck to talking about the incident last night? Didn't the reporter know she would be as concerned about the animals' well-being as he seemed to be?

Instead he made it sound like she was involved in something huge—and incredibly wrong.

Growing up, she'd had a reputation for being the kid who always talked about animals, who brought them home to take care of. She'd spent countless hours at the zoo as a kid, watching the previous zookeeper—Zane Ford—do his work. She'd learned so much from him. Could he really have been involved in exotic animal trading? It was almost unconscionable. He'd loved the animals. Yes, he'd also been concerned about money, but she'd thought that was because he needed it to feed and care for the animals adequately.

She'd grieved when she heard he'd been lost

in the flood. Could he really have been deceiving everyone? Selling animals?

Sam barked once. Elise turned back to the house. She needed to tell Jonah about the newspaper article.

The mailbox clanged. She looked back to find it had imploded, struck with something small that had torn through the metal. The sound of a gunshot echoed across the hill.

Sam's paws collided with her before she even realized someone was shooting at her.

FIVE

"Stay in the barn." Jonah yelled the command to Nathan over his shoulder and flew out the barn door. It wasn't the gunshot that propelled him down the drive. Those were common enough in his line of work—though not usually this close to his house. It was Elise's scream.

He pulled his gun as he ran, glad he hadn't decided to forgo wearing it at home because of Nathan and Elise. Their possible discomfort at his having a gun on his person was less important than the danger they were in.

Danger that had now visited his doorstep.

Sam barked but didn't move. It looked like he was sitting on something at the mailbox. Or some*one*.

Jonah slipped his phone from his pocket and held it to his ear. "Call emergency dispatch."

The phone rang and immediately connected. "Nine-one-one, what is your emergency?"

"Shots fired." He gave his credentials and his address.

"Units are on their way."

Jonah hung up and stowed the phone. He was close enough he could see the person on the ground under Sam was Elise. "Sam, stay."

Elise lifted her head. "Jonah!"

She shifted to get up, so Jonah yelled again, "Stay down."

Elise stilled, and Sam lowered his head, his ears still pricked. Jonah could see in the dog's eyes that he was fully alert. "Don't move." This time the command was for both of them.

Jonah crouched beside her, checking her visually for injuries.

Eyes full of fear, Elise looked up at him. "Where's Nathan?"

"In the barn. What happened?"

"Someone shot at me and Sam tackled me to the ground."

Jonah surveyed the area, his gaze lighting on the destroyed mailbox. Large caliber, a rifle round most likely. He took in the tree line, and his neighbor's house and barn. The shooter could be waiting in any of the spots that would've provided cover. If he'd even stuck around after firing.

He rubbed Sam's neck. "Good dog." The old army dog nuzzled his hand.

"Can I get up? The ground is kind of hard."

Jonah looked around again. He could hear police sirens in the distance, so he stowed his weapon in the holster on his hip.

The shots had ceased after that first burst, but it didn't mean they shouldn't be cautious. He needed to get Elise inside.

Jonah directed Sam with a command to get off Elise and at least give her some relief from the dog's weight. Two sheriff's cars pulled up on the blacktop, and the deputies climbed out, drawing their weapons.

"Anyone hurt?"

Jonah shook his head. Satisfied the danger was no longer imminent, he helped Elise up. Dirt was smeared down the front of the clothes he'd left out for her. The sight of her in his favorite T-shirt struck a pang in him that he'd been unprepared for.

The sheriff's car pulled up behind the other cars. Two more cars, local police from town, came into view also. This was turning out to be a regular circus.

When the deputies strode over, he said, "These officers will take you inside." He glanced at them. "Ask your questions there."

They strode away, and Sam's head shifted. Nathan was peeking out of the barn, so Jonah waved him toward Elise and the officers. When they were level with the barn, he emerged to walk with them inside.

The reality that Elise had been fired upon hit Jonah then, the feeling so profound he rubbed the flat of his hand across his chest. She'd only been back in his life since yesterday, and he could have lost her.

He strode to his house, Sam in tow.

Elise was just about to settle herself on the couch, and the detectives hadn't asked her anything yet. One was bringing her a cup of water.

Jonah stopped just inside the living room. "Why did you walk to the mailbox?"

Elise turned to him then, eyes wide. He should regret being sharp with her, but she should have had more care with her safety. "I was getting the paper. There's an article about—"

"You didn't know that. You walked out in the open and put yourself in serious danger. Why didn't you stay inside, Elise?"

Nathan shifted like he was readying himself to protect his mom. The cops just held their ground. They knew Jonah well enough to know he didn't lose his temper easily—or for no reason. In the close-knit community of local law enforcement, news about Elise's arrival was going to get around fast.

Elise stuck her hands on her hips. "I didn't

know I was going to get shot at! How could I have?"

"You knew you were in danger."

"Yeah, but in your *driveway*?" She blew out a breath and put her arm around her waist, hugging herself. Her face twisted as angry tears filled her eyes. "I didn't know I would get shot at."

Jonah blew out a breath, trying not to let her emotions prick his conscience. "I have to go talk to the Sheriff."

Elise stared out Jonah's living room window, trying to purge the feeling of having been thoroughly dismissed. She knew why he'd yelled. He'd always gotten loud when he was scared, always. How loud he got was directly related to how scared he was. Which meant Jonah had been really, really worried about her getting hurt. A fact that comforted her, even as she was angry he'd basically blamed her for almost getting hurt.

"Ms. Tanner?"

She turned to the cop, Detective William Manners, but she didn't sit when he motioned her to. The man was older, probably in his sixties, and had gray stubble on his jaw. "You want to tell me why you think you're being targeted all of a sudden?"

She'd filled him in on the zoo, and her brother. It wouldn't have looked good if the sheriff's department found out later she was Fix Tanner's sister—even if they'd had no contact. But now, looking at the sheriff's deputy and the disapproving look on his face, all the decades-old shame over the trailer where she'd lived, the state her mom lived in and her brother's antics welled up in her.

Jonah and Martin had repeatedly told her it didn't matter what she'd grown up with, that it didn't stain her. But a lifetime of people looking down on where she'd come from had affected her. She wasn't naive enough to think otherwise.

"No, I don't know why I'm being targeted. The only thing I can think of is that whoever stole the files thinks I can identify him, and so he tried to kill me today."

Could it have something to do with the newspaper article? How did the reporter know all that about the zookeeper? Zane Ford couldn't have been caught up in exotic animal trading, could he? She found it hard to believe he would do that to animals he'd dedicated his life to taking care of.

If the man wasn't dead, she'd have been able to ask him.

"We'd like you to come in to the station today

and look at mug shots, to see if you can identify the man who bombed the office."

Elise nodded. "The police asked me the same thing, I'll make sure to do that. Do you think it was the same man in the office who set the bomb?" She wasn't convinced, but what did she know? She wasn't a cop.

The cop said, "We're looking for conclusive evidence that will prove one way or another."

The cops excused themselves, and Elise turned again to the window. Nathan stood talking with the US marshals who had tried to arrest him last night. Jonah looked like he was coordinating a search-and-rescue operation that was going to encompass the entire area while she was closeted in the house. All because she wanted fresh air and to read the newspaper.

Jonah might still care about her, but only to make sure his friend, the girl he considered his little sister, was okay. That was all. She didn't blame him for wanting to get to know Nathan, and to keep her safe for her son's sake. But the ache in her chest was because he didn't seem to want to be around her. Her younger self had suffered a debilitating crush on Jonah. He'd been so strong in her eyes, the perfect answer to her childhood dream of being rescued from her life. Too bad that dream was over now.

After Jonah had left for the marines, never

even responding to her letters or the packages she sent, Elise had allowed that dream to die. Despite his assertions of how much he cared for her, Jonah had obviously been content to let their friendship languish.

In the end, it had been Martin who offered her everything she'd ever wanted. But now he was gone, too. All she had left was Nathan.

Elise needed to remember that.

Deputy Marshal Hailey Shelder motioned to the house using Jonah's newspaper. "The deputies left. They want your girl to look at mug shots before lunch."

"Thanks." The mug-shot binder was more like multiple thick folders, so Jonah figured that would take the rest of the day. He'd have to find cover to watch Nathan and Elise before and after then. He couldn't blow off a whole day of work, even if it was related to a case. Fix Tanner was one of many open cases he had right now, and the stuff going on with Elise wasn't conclusively related.

"What do you make of the article?"

Shelder's mouth moved side to side while she thought. She never did go completely still, not even when most people would freeze. "I think the reporter either got the information himself or got it from whoever was in the office."

"Find a picture of the reporter—"

"And show it to Elise." Shelder stepped away, pulling out her phone. "Good idea."

Jonah glanced at the house as Shelder strode down the drive. He ignored the fact that his house looked weathered, badly in need of fixing up, and saw Elise at the window. Looking at him.

She was like a magnet, drawing him to her. Elise had always been like that, and Jonah had given up fighting the pull of her a long time ago and left town instead. She'd been far too young to consider a relationship with, and when he returned the next time she'd been married to Martin. But just because her presence had the same effect on him even all these years later didn't mean he had to do something about it. She was his weakness. He'd known that the minute he found out she'd left, and it was as if his heart had been removed from his chest. She'd walked away with it…to Idaho of all places. So near, all these years, and yet she might as well have been on another planet.

If she could identify the man from the zoo it would go a ways toward wrapping this up. He didn't like the idea of her being in danger.

Nathan glanced over and gave Jonah a tentative smile, like the kid was waiting for something else to go wrong. Or explode. He knew how Nathan felt, but Jonah was going to figure this out.

All he had to do was convince Elise to listen—and actually follow instructions. He didn't blame her for doing something as innocuous as going to the mailbox, but he would have felt a whole lot better if he'd gone with her. Although if he'd done that, Nathan would have wound up in the middle of sniper fire along with the rest of them.

"Quite the hoo-hah this morning. Eh, Rivers?" Jonah's elderly neighbor strode up to him, holding his hand out. The man was late seventies easily, but walked his land every day and ate fresh from his garden. He was probably healthier than Jonah would ever be.

"You could say that, Tucker." Jonah motioned Nathan over. When the teenager reached them, Jonah said, "Tucker, this is my nephew, Nathan. Nathan, this is my neighbor. Tucker was army, like your dad."

Nathan brightened up, shaking the old man's hand. "Nice to meet you."

Making the connection aloud, it dawned on Jonah—Tucker had the skills to have shot Jonah's mailbox. And the hardware. The man had more guns in his house than Jonah had seen in his life, but Tucker's prize possession was his old sniper rifle.

"What have you been up to this morning, Tucker?" He often made small talk with the vet when they crossed paths. Hopefully he wouldn't know that today Jonah's question was not so innocuous.

"Not much. Manny's laid up, so I only made a short walk this morning."

Tucker's dog was a husky, and an old one at that. Manny had a lot of health problems Tucker had told him about—in depth. If the dog was having a bad morning, Jonah believed Tucker would stay close to home.

Jonah didn't know why he felt that Tucker could have been involved. There wasn't evidence to justify his assertion, but the theory wouldn't leave him alone, and Jonah had learned to trust his instincts. It was only when he ignored his gut that bad things happened. Like getting shot in the middle of a manhunt.

He rubbed a hand across his flat stomach where the ache seemed to ebb and flow for no reason. "Nathan and I should be getting inside. I was showing him my bike, so we didn't have breakfast."

Tucker's eyes lit up. "You keep me posted when that thing's finished."

"Sure, Tucker." Like Jonah was actually contemplating parting with it when it was done. Not likely. The last hold he had on Martin's memory wasn't something he could put a monetary value on.

Tucker walked away and Nathan turned to him. "You're going to sell the bike?"

"No way." Jonah eyed the kid. "I'd give the thing to you before I sold it to anyone else."

Nathan's eyes lit up. "Serious?"

Jonah realized the implication of what he'd said. "Or you could borrow it sometime." He nudged Nathan's shoulder.

"Or *you* could borrow it." Nathan shoved his shoulder back.

Jonah sobered. "Where do you think you'll be after the summer?"

Nathan shrugged. "I got accepted into a zoology program at the university, so I'll be leaving in August and it'll be nothing but labs and research classes for four years."

Jonah eyed him. "You like all that science stuff?"

"Sure." Nathan shrugged. "Maybe I'll enjoy it."

Multiple thoughts went through Jonah's head, but he didn't know either Nathan or Elise well enough to speculate on the topic of Nathan's future.

The front door slammed open. Shelder was already down the porch steps with Elise on her heels when the screen door snapped back on its hinges.

"She identified him." Shelder stopped in front of him. "It's the reporter."

Jonah turned to Elise. "Are you sure? It won't be official until you make the identification to the police, but it'll give us something to go on."

Elise nodded. "That man on Hailey's phone—" She motioned to Shelder's cell. Jonah saw the reporter's picture was on the screen.

"That's the man who hit me in the office."

SIX

Elise's heart was still pounding at the revelation of the identity of the man who'd attacked her in the office and stolen files. A silver Buick pulled onto the drive and crawled past cops searching the area, gathering evidence and taking Jonah's mailbox into custody. Or that was what it looked like, at least. The driver lifted his hand to the cops, who nodded respectfully in return.

Jonah rubbed his hand along his jaw, his eyes on the newcomer. Elise figured the gesture probably didn't mean he just found out he had a math test second period he hadn't studied for. She had no frame of reference for Jonah's mannerisms now. "Who is that?"

Shelder—who'd asked Elise to call her Hailey—was the one who answered, "The mayor."

Elise caught her tone. "You don't like him?"

The mayor had been completely professional in their emails and the one conversation they'd had over the phone. Essentially she'd been hired sight unseen. But still, he'd been pleasant enough and there hadn't been any other qualified candidates.

"It isn't that. It's the office itself I don't have such an affinity for." Shelder shot her a wry smile. "Dominic Alvarez is a perfectly nice retiree with too much time on his hands, who wanted to help the town after the flood."

"He didn't get elected?"

"Loosely."

Elise wondered what the rest of the story was, but there wasn't time to answer before the elderly Hispanic man parked his car and hopped out. His hair was perfectly arranged and his suit included a buttoned waistcoat. "Ms. Tanner?"

Elise strode over and stuck her hand out. "It's nice to meet you finally, Mr. Alvarez."

He held her hand with both of his, his hands warm where hers had been cold from what Hailey told her was shock. The cordiality in his dark brown eyes was genuine. "I'd planned to visit with you this morning, but my assistant informed me of what happened yesterday and this morning. Are you okay?"

"Yes, thank you." He released her hand, and Elise waved Nathan over so she could introduce her son.

The mayor shook Nathan's hand and waved toward the house. "Should we go inside? There's a chill out here, and you probably want a moment to sit."

Elise didn't want to spend much more time out in the open, even if the area was crawling with law enforcement. Not when she could still hear the echo of the gunshot in her ears. She nodded and the mayor stepped closer, holding out his elbow. She slipped her arm in his and he patted her hand as though they were walking through stately gardens, not the dirt drive that led to Jonah's house.

Sam trotted over to the mayor. Dominic bent to scratch the dog's ears. "Good dog."

Elise wasn't used to people being so concerned about her—it was almost disconcerting. The introvert in her needed some quiet time. Maybe she could go to the ranch where a few of the animals were being cared for and spend some time with them, instead of using all her time rebuilding the zoo. She'd have to ask the mayor about that.

Alvarez waved Nathan over, and her son walked with them. Elise heard Hailey chuckle, but didn't get the chance to find out what was so funny. Jonah stood in front of them. Was he going to move, or would they have to swerve around him?

"Good morning, son."

Jonah didn't move. "Dom."

Elise said, "Do…you guys know each other?"

Jonah turned to the mayor. "Elise had a scare. She doesn't need to be working right now." His eyes were dark with something she didn't understand.

"I know that. This isn't about work. I'll go easy on her."

"Dom—"

The mayor glanced at her. "Come." He walked her around a now sullen Jonah toward the house, as though he'd been here many times and was perfectly at home. "Let's go sit."

When they were a short distance from Jonah, Elise looked back. He was watching them walk. The mayor looked back over his shoulder. "Is the coffeepot on, Jonah?"

"Yeah, Dom. The coffee's on."

The mayor—Dom, evidently, to his friends— leaned close to her as they walked. "Jonah is my stepson."

Elise nearly tripped. "You're married to…"

"Nettie, yes. For four years now." Dom grinned. "I heard a rumor that makes you my step-daughter-in-law." Before Elise had a chance to answer, he turned to Nathan. "And you, my step-grandson."

Nathan smiled. "I guess so."

The kid had never had so much family in his whole life as he'd had in the last two days. He was probably on overload. Elise sure was.

She bit her lip. "You really married Bernadette Rivers?"

Dom's gaze on her softened. "She's told me so much about you, Elise. Nettie very much... Well, none of it is for me to say, given Nettie is the one who needs to make amends. But she greatly regrets the wrong done to you."

"Because she found out she has a grandson?"

Jonah must have called his mom the night before, after Elise fell asleep, and told her all about Nathan. She glanced back at Jonah, but he was talking with Hailey. Was he going to leave, to go talk with the reporter she'd just identified as the man who'd attacked her in the zoo office?

Maybe he would just go without telling her, assuming she would be fine without him. Which, of course, was true. She didn't need it to be specifically *him* who made sure nobody else tried to kill her this weekend. Any of the marshals, or a cop, or Sam, would do.

She reached down and patted the dog and then turned back to Dom. "All of a sudden Bernadette wants to make amends?"

They stopped at the porch. Elise opened her mouth to tell the mayor where his wife—Elise's former mother-in-law—could go, but he cut her off.

"You're probably not feeling up to this. Please don't get upset. That was not my intention." His mouth compressed into a frown. "I shouldn't have mentioned it, but I didn't want there to be secrets between us."

Nathan opened the front door for them. Elise poured the coffee and they sat on the couch where she'd been interviewed by the police only minutes ago. Jonah didn't come in, but what did she care? At least she was trying not to. Whether he was inside with her or outside shouldn't matter so much. She didn't need to be that attuned to his presence in her life...or her heart.

Elise's cup shook, so she set it down on the table. "Thank you for coming to check on me. I really appreciate it." She covered the shakes by clasping her knees tight. Her smile probably looked brittle, but it was the best she could come up with. If she'd eaten lunch she would probably be losing it, but her stomach was now painfully empty.

Nathan left the room silently.

Dom waited until Nathan had left the room. "Your son might favor his father." He smiled. "But he reminds me of his uncle."

Thinking about her son, Elise's heart unclenched just a little. She couldn't lose it, not when Nathan was relying on her to be the parent. Sure, he was almost grown, but that didn't mean there weren't times he needed his mom. She'd recognized as much in the hospital.

He strode back into the room and handed her a banana. "Here, eat this."

Was it that obvious? He did know her better than anyone in the world. And where once that had been true of Jonah and Martin, now the position of most important in her life went to Nathan. *God, thank You for keeping me safe today.* They needed each other equally, and she could easily have been killed if she hadn't taken that step away from the mailbox at just the right time.

Dom glanced between them. "Well, let's talk zoo. Shall we?"

Elise nodded. Talking about the animals would take her mind off the craziness of the last two days.

At least until the next crazy thing happened.

Shelder hung up the phone. "Parker and Ames are ready to roll. They'll meet us at Colombes's place."

Jonah was itching to go after the reporter and find out if it really was him who had attacked Elise.

He wanted to look at the house where Dom had walked with Elise, and where his traitorous dog had disappeared, but he didn't. Hailey would know, and Jonah would never live down pining for a person of interest in one of their cases.

"I take it there's nothing new on the hunt for Fix." Especially not when the team was raring to go after the reporter. Why were they all of a sudden so concerned with Elise's well-being?

"Parker and Ames are still trying to get an address on the girlfriend from Eric's research. Two they tried this morning turned out to be previous residences, and no one seems to know where she or Fix is living now. Eric isn't coming up with much else."

And now someone had opened fire on Elise.

Shelder said, "Was it really a sniper?"

"Looks like it."

"Anyone you know?"

Jonah remembered the thought that had crossed his mind when his neighbor came over to talk with him and Elise. The man was retired army, and had the necessary skills. At least from what he'd told Jonah. "What did the investigators get?"

"They're still looking for the bullet. It tore a hole through the mailbox, so they're tracking where it might've gone. They'll find it eventually."

He'd have made sure to use a bullet that couldn't be traced back to him. If they did find it, the likelihood that it would lead to an arrest was slim. But they still had to try.

Shelder continued. "Local police are talking to all your neighbors. They've got a decent lock on the area he'd have to have been in to hit your mailbox at that angle."

Jonah looked at the thing. It was mangled so bad he wondered that they could use it to work the angle of trajectory back to the location where the shooter would have to have been situated. "I need you to stay here and watch Elise and Nathan."

Shelder reacted. "Because I'm a girl?"

Jonah shot her a look. "You're the only team member here, and I'm going after this reporter."

"You got a chance to read the article?" She didn't comment on the fact that it wasn't their case to investigate, and he was grateful. The police knew he was invested now, since the threat had been brought to his doorstep. They were going to have to let him do what he needed to do to take care of Elise and Nathan.

Jonah nodded. "I think Howard Colombes is the one who broke into the office. But I'm leaning away from him being the one who planted the bomb. I think he was just looking for a story. I think he knew who Elise was when he saw her in the office and took the opportunity to take her keys."

"Pretty vicious attack for a story."

"Maybe he thought she was in on it. Selling animals." The reporter could also be an animal-rights activist. It would make for a strong drive to uncover cruelty or mistreatment of animals."

"If you want to go, I can tell Elise where you went."

Jonah saw the look on Shelder's face. "I can tell her myself."

She raised both hands, palms out. "Sure, boss. Whatever you say."

"I stand behind what I said yesterday. I'm not above firing you, Shelder."

Shelder sobered in a moment of empathy. "She's had a rough couple of days. Add in you on top of it and she's probably got something akin to whiplash."

"What do you mean, add in me?"

She motioned toward him, shoulders to shoes. "You can be...intimidating."

"Elise and I, and Martin, we were best friends."

"In childhood, yeah." Shelder paused a beat. "But I bet you're a lot different than your teen-age self. Taller. Bigger. You're the boss and you know it. A woman like Elise has had to hold her whole world together for years. She's dealt with her husband's death, the birth of her baby, made a name for herself in her career and now she's made a big change. Coming home. Running into you probably wasn't part of the plan for her first day back."

Jonah's gut churned. "Or getting hurt, or shot at this morning."

"I'm just saying, give her some time to get used to you again."

Jonah was willing to concede that his colleague knew what she was talking about. Hailey was a single mom herself, also taking care of her aging father. He was suddenly glad she had fallen in love with Eric Hanning. He also recognized a surge of hope. Hailey was a strong, independent woman, and yet she'd learned how to rely on Eric for help in a tough situation.

Could Elise do that?

It was tempting to assume he was someone she wanted in her life now, but he couldn't know that. If he wanted her to get used to him again, he had to ease her into it gently. That plan was certain to produce better results than the force of his will. Jonah had waited plenty long enough to feel that spark again—the spark he'd only ever felt with little Elise.

Despite the difference in their ages, Jonah had seen something in her even as a teenager. Puppy love, maybe. But it was strong enough that he'd retreated to the military while he waited for her to finish growing up. Then she'd gone and married Martin instead.

Now was his second chance, and Jonah wasn't willing to step wrong and live another lifetime without her. He'd waited this long—he could wait a little longer.

Inside, Elise was on the couch with a banana peel on the coffee table in front of her. Jonah saw how pale she was, and he crouched to brush some hair back from the side of her face. "You okay?"

Her brown eyes were wide, like a doe's.

"I have to go talk with the reporter, but Hailey's going to stay here."

"Okay." Her voice was small, like the young Elise he'd known. She cleared her throat. "That's fine."

"Maybe Nathan could make you some tea or something. Do you still drink hot tea?"

She nodded, then looked aside at her son. "Yes, please."

"I'll be back soon." Jonah wanted to kiss her forehead, the way he'd done many times years before, but he held back. Affection wasn't what she needed, or wanted, from him now.

He drove across town with the radio off, wondering at how much his life had changed in only a day. He'd been on a lonely trajectory, nothing but work and a little family in his mom and Dom. Now Elise had brought her light back into his life.

And Jonah was going to find out who was trying to kill her.

He pulled up down the street from Howard Colombes's house, donned his vest and grabbed his shotgun from the lockbox in his trunk. Parker, Ames and Hanning met him on the sidewalk. Parker led Hanning to the backyard while Ames backed up Jonah at the front door.

Jonah knocked and it swung open.

They cleared the rooms from front to back, meeting in the middle. Jonah headed to the center room in the hallway. When he opened the door, he saw it was an office, and Howard Colombes was in his chair.

Dead.

SEVEN

Beyond the body, the reporter's wall safe was open and empty. Howard Colombes had been shot in the forehead, execution-style. His desk was clear except for the computer monitor, and the tower under the desk had been unplugged and removed. The file-cabinet drawers were open and someone had cleaned out Howard's papers.

Jonah finished up his notes and put his phone back in his pocket. He passed the two homicide detectives the police department had sent, and met his guys in the hall.

Parker's eyes were dark, the way they always were when he was faced with death. The former navy SEAL kept his past pretty well hidden, but Jonah saw the darkness creep up when their work turned grisly.

Ames was all mouth, and usually at the wrong moment. But he was working on it.

Eric Hanning was the newcomer of the

group. Formerly assigned to witness protection, he came to the hunt for each fugitive with a more cerebral approach. And he was excellent at research.

"So, what do we have?"

The three men were used to his testing approach to a hunt. He wasn't going to spoonfeed them everything, not when one of them would likely be team leader soon. He was sure Parker would take the position when Jonah transitioned to a more office-based role, but he didn't want to give it up just yet.

Jonah glanced at Parker, who said, "Whoever planted the bomb is cleaning up after himself. Howard Colombes was a loose end, someone who knew too much about what was going on at the zoo before it flooded. Whoever has a vested interest in the story not coming out is getting rid of anyone who knows."

"Which means he isn't going to stop until Elise is dead, too."

"But by that logic, everyone who read the article in the paper should be killed," Eric said.

Ames shook his head. "Not since he's destroying evidence. The article is only hearsay if there's no evidence to corroborate the story."

Jonah nodded. "That means there's something about Elise that's put her on his list."

"Did she know about the animal trading?"

Parker's eyebrow rose. "Maybe from when she was here years ago?"

Jonah said, "She did work at the zoo. Maybe she knows something, or might remember something. It doesn't have to be simply her being hired back that's the reason she's being targeted now."

"Guess you should find out."

Jonah shook his head at Parker's cynicism. Some woman had clearly burned him if he was this distrusting of any female he met. Jonah would have asked him who she was, but they didn't talk about their personal lives.

"So, who looks good for this?"

Eric said, "The zookeeper was killed in the flood. The few employees of the zoo found jobs elsewhere. There wasn't much call for their skills after the zoo was destroyed, and a lot of the staff were volunteers, anyway. The vet moved his practice across town, but he apparently still works with the zoo's animals at the sanctuary and even houses a few at his own practice. The rest were transferred out of town for the time being."

"We should go talk to him. If he's not the one causing all this, he could be in danger also."

Jonah agreed with Parker's assessment. "You and Ames take the vet. Hanning, go meet up with Shelder and cover Elise. I'm going to head in to the office after I coordinate with local police on their investigation into Colombes's death. They need to know what we suspect happened. I'll work on locating Fix Tanner."

There wasn't anyone else connected with the zoo who was still around. And yet someone was trying to bury information—and people. Who was so intent on keeping their secret that they blew up the zoo office and then tried to shoot Elise in broad daylight? Sniper training and the ability to kill with a single, accurate shot.

Was there anyone previously associated with the zoo who hunted or was ex-military?

Jonah spoke with the cops working the scene and then excused himself. As he was walking out, his phone rang.

"Yeah, Mom?"

"You're busy." Bernadette Rivers had always had perfect diction. She'd despaired over her sons' rambunctious behavior, and hadn't particularly approved of either of them going into the military. That was his father's influence, encouraging them to do something honorable that challenged them and at the same time meant they gained self-respect. Too bad he never got to see them do it, as he'd died when Jonah was in high school.

"It's fine." He walked out of the house, down the street to his car.

"Uh… I heard about Elise."

The statement was telling in itself, given the fact his mom never hesitated about anything. "I know you've heard that she's back in town."

"How is she?"

There was no surprise over Elise's return, only concern? His mom had never once thought to keep her opinion of Elise to herself.

"She was freaked out, last time I saw her." He'd seen that wide-eyed stare of Elise's many times, when her mom went on one of her drinking binges. He didn't like it now any more than he had then.

"Maybe I should come by, bring a casserole or something. She's staying with you, right?"

His mother wanted to bring Elise a casserole?

"I know you probably want to meet Nathan. He's a great kid, Mom, but he's probably also overwhelmed. They've been here less than two days and already his mom's almost been killed twice." The teenager seemed to be handling it well enough, but was he going to share with Jonah if he wasn't? "You should probably wait a few days, give Elise some time to settle and find her feet." To heal.

Dom had already spent time with her. So why did Jonah feel the need to keep her to himself for the time being? Elise needed to be the one to decide if she even wanted to see Jonah's mom or not. They'd never gotten along—the debutante and the girl from the trailer—both with a chip on their shoulder. It didn't get better after Elise had married Martin. Jonah's brother hadn't worried over the tension between his wife and mother; he'd simply left them to figure out their differences.

Now was apparently a different story. For some reason—he was guessing Nathan had a lot to do with it—his mom wanted to make amends.

Bernadette Rivers sighed. "If you think that's best, I'll abide by your wishes."

"Thank you."

"Dom said she didn't look too good. You're probably right."

His mom usually wouldn't have taken someone else's feelings into account. She'd been different lately, and it wasn't just since she'd married Dom. She was softer now. He liked the change, even while he didn't really understand what had happened to her.

"What's up with you lately, Mom?"

He heard a sound, like a gasp. "I've been waiting for you to ask, honey. Can I tell you? Is that okay?"

"Sure, Mom. Tell me."

"I'm so happy you've noticed. That's what I wanted. Not just to make this decision and then tell everyone before I knew what it meant, or how to really live it. I've been born again, Jonah. Like your father always talked about." She laughed. "It was Dom who brought me to church, and now I've made a decision to be a Christian, because God loves me so much, what else can I do but follow Him?"

Her excitement was infectious. "That's great, Mom." He didn't totally understand it, not when his adulthood had found him on a different path, and he struggled with the faith he'd once placed so much importance on. Perhaps her experience would help him find his feet again.

But later. Right now Jonah had a woman to protect, and more than one man to find.

Elise waited for Hailey to open her door. The marshal scanned the area, one hand on the gun on her hip, while Elise climbed out of the car. It had been Nathan's suggestion that they come to the ranch and check on the bigger animals.

"I called ahead. Sienna's ready for us."

Elise smoothed down the bottom of her jacket. "Okay."

Sienna was a fairly new resident who loved animals and didn't live far from the zoo, but far enough that her property had been above the water line and she'd been able to buy the house when most people were rebuilding. She'd volunteered to house the animals long-term until the zoo was back up and running. And her place was close enough to the zoo that Elise could check on the animals frequently.

She could see the zoo, and its destruction, from the hill where Sienna's ranch was.

Elise, Hailey, Nathan and Eric trailed past an old, nasty red pickup that looked like it didn't even run. A striking woman dressed in skinny jeans, knee-high cowgirl boots and a lumberjack shirt strode around the house. Her eyes darted between them, obviously nervous at the influx of newcomers. Elise knew how she felt.

She gave Sienna an unobtrusive wave. "Hi, I'm Elise."

Sienna smiled wide and stuck out her hand. "Nice to meet ya." Her accent was thick Boston, but she looked like any other country girl in Oregon.

"How are the animals?"

"Oh, they're fine." Sienna waved them all toward a barn. "Someone's been eating Train's food, and Eleanor seems like she has a cold or something. The vet is due any minute to look at her."

"Great." Elise was glad they were being taken care of. It took a load off her shoulders that she didn't have to supervise the cleanup and rebuilding at the same time as taking care of the animals. They needed their long-term home back.

Sienna pulled the barn door open. Warming lamps had been set up for the turtle in its enclosure. Farther down, the minihorse with a cold, Eleanor, stood beside the llama, Francis. Both eyed their visitors until Nathan pulled two apples from his pockets. The teenager always had snacks on him for the animals; she should've known he'd bring some from Jonah's house.

Eric stopped several feet behind them to pull out his phone. Elise watched him type a message and then slide the cell back into his pocket before he took up a station by the door. She understood they were protecting her, and she wasn't going to be ungrateful. But she also wasn't used to it and didn't know if she ever would be.

"I also keep spotting the tiger, Shera."

Elise spun back to Sienna. "Seriously?" She had no idea the tiger who'd escaped from the zoo was the same old, blind Bengal that had lived there years ago when she volunteered. "Shera's still alive?"

Sienna grinned. "I've heard all about the old gal. Figured she's pretty hungry, so I keep leaving out some raw steak. Spotted her creeping along the fence line a couple of times, so I left the gate open when the horses were inside. Food was eaten, but I haven't seen her up close. I'm not even sure if I want to."

"She's pretty harmless, since she has no teeth. And she's too old to hunt. But just a swat with one paw could do some serious damage. She can get berries, and fruit, but she'll favor deer. She'll probably stay clear of most other animals."

"Good to know."

A deep-throated truck pulled up outside. Minutes later the zoo's vet strode in, carrying a medical bag. His gray hair was covered by a cowboy hat, and his mustache twitched at the sight of all of them. "Quite the crowd for one mini."

Sienna introduced them all, and Elise got to visit with the minihorse while the vet did his examination. She could have diagnosed the animal's sinus infection herself, but it was nice to have a licensed professional on hand. It wasn't worth her missing something more serious.

While the vet did the treatment, Nathan distracted the antsy llama.

That was how Jonah found them, surrounded by furred creatures and stepping in animal droppings in a barn that might smell bad to most people—but to Elise, it smelled like safety.

Jonah's gaze didn't even stop on them, zeroing in on the vet instead. "I'll need a word outside when you're done." He folded his arms, and the vet—seeing his seriousness—nodded.

"Is there a problem?" Sienna looked suddenly nervous.

Elise shot her a reassuring smile. "Jonah's an old friend. He's helping me out with a problem right now."

"Good friends are hard to find."

Elise nodded, wondering at the obvious pain underneath her words. She looked at Jonah. "Everything okay?"

Hailey said, "I thought Parker and Ames were covering the vet."

Jonah lifted his chin to her. "They're checking a possible address on Fix. I traded with them."

Elise studied the man before her. He glanced over, and his brow twitched. Apparently the two of them hadn't lost the connection they'd had years ago, which didn't require any words to be spoken for them to communicate.

Jonah smiled. "Doing better?"

He knew how she felt about caring for animals, or just being around them and spending time with them. "Nathan had a good idea."

Her son grinned his father's smile. "It's been known to happen."

The smile dredged up long-buried memories. She'd had a heady teenage crush on both Rivers brothers, but after Jonah left and broke her heart she'd found love with Martin. Then her husband had done his best to make his big brother proud and joined the army. Jonah had cost her the two best friendships in her life, not to mention her husband's future—their life together. Her husband's need to live up to his older brother had cost her son his father.

However much Jonah wanted to rekindle some kind of rapport, or a friendship, she wasn't going to let that happen. No matter how much their connection was still there. She would happily concede the fact that he was capable of protecting her from harm, but he'd never protected her heart.

"Whoa." Eric ducked inside and slid the door shut. "There's a tiger outside. I'm not even kidding."

Jonah's face washed white. Elise laughed and turned to the vet. "If you'll excuse me, I'll be reconnecting with an old friend. Only, could I borrow some tranquilizer?"

"I don't have a gun. Only a needle."

"I should be able to get close enough for that." It was risky, but if she was presented the opportunity she'd do it. She'd rather it was her and not a kid out biking who ran into the aging tiger.

Elise took the full needle and made for the door. Nathan fell into step beside her. "I'll help."

Elise stopped at the door. "Wouldn't miss it for the world."

"No. No way. I don't think so." Jonah strode over. "There's a tiger out there? We need to call animal control."

"They haven't managed to catch her so far." Elise bit back the snort. "Animal control will have no clue what to do with a tiger. I do. And so does Nathan."

"Isn't it dangerous?"

"It'll be more dangerous to other people if we keep letting her roam all over the place. Shera could hurt someone." Elise didn't wait for him to argue more. She just slid the door open and slid it closed behind her, dismissing Jonah.

"Elise—" His shout was muffled by the barn door. And so was the female laughing—either Sienna or Hailey or both. The two women could quickly become Elise's friends, if she had any free time outside the zoo to spend with them.

She scanned the area as she walked. When the barn door slid open, she looked back to see Jonah emerge with his gun out.

"No way." She stopped and turned to him.
"You cannot shoot this animal."

"I'm not here to protect you from the tiger.
This is to protect you from the person trying
to kill *you*."

EIGHT

Elise lifted a charred piece of wood and tossed it aside. All that fuss at Sienna's ranch and they hadn't even found Shera. Now it was getting dark and the old tiger was probably cold, and hungry. Then she'd had to look at photos to officially identify the reporter, even though he was dead.

She threw another piece of wood, narrowly missing Jonah.

"Watch out, Lise." His eyes narrowed, but there was a hint of humor there as he turned to her. "What did I do now?"

He looked so boyish, Elise couldn't help laughing. Then it wouldn't stop. She set her hands on her knees and bent over, trying to suck in air.

"Uh-oh. It's never good when you get all hysterical."

Nathan chuckled, across the entrance pathway, clearing his side. "She's snapped."

Elise straightened. "I have not. But if I had, it would be entirely justified." She put a hand on her side. "Ouch, my ribs hurt."

Jonah crossed the distance between them, and she noted Nathan and the marshals all strategically turning away. Did they think something was going on between Elise and Jonah? Because there most certainly was not.

"Are you okay?"

"What?" Elise jumped, and turned to him. "Uh, fine. Thanks."

Jonah reached up and tugged on the growing-out strand of her bangs. "No bruises from the mailbox incident?"

Elise shook her head. She didn't think she could talk. Jonah had done that pulling-on-her-hair thing when she was a teenager, but it hadn't felt like this. Serious crush or not, Jonah back then had nothing on the grown-up version.

Jonah stepped back, his face awash with mischief. "You should get back to work. There's a lot to do."

Elise narrowed her eyes. If he wanted to stick around for the hauling and sweating part, what was it to her? She knew he was primarily here to protect her, but he could have claimed that meant he needed to be watching and not working. Yet here he was. Still as honorable as ever.

She swiped her notepad from her backpack

and started making a list. They could clear debris, but soon enough they would need a construction crew with heavy equipment to remove what was unusable. After that the crew would have to start reconstruction of the buildings and the animal enclosures. There was a lot that had to be done before the zoo could reopen, but this would help her start making a list on paper.

Jonah looked aside at her. "Can I ask you a favor? I was thinking maybe you know some people Fix used to hang out with. Anyone I wouldn't know to talk to."

Elise tried to think if there were friends of her brother who might still be in town. "I don't know how I'm supposed to know who is here and who isn't."

"What about your mom? Could she have stayed in contact with Fix? Did she ever mention him?"

She stilled. "Are you working right now?"

Jonah shook his head. "I don't know what you mean."

"I mean, you're interrogating me. You want information, so you're working *me* right now."

"Elise—"

"For your information, I have not once in the whole of Nathan's life said one word to my mother. Apart from the fact that her trailer never had a phone, and I haven't been back here, I don't see how you'd think I would even keep in contact with that woman." She sucked in a breath. "You know, Jonah. Of all people, you know."

His gaze dropped, and why not? Jonah had been driving the truck half the times they'd had to pick her mom up from whatever bar she'd passed out in. Fix had always been conveniently too busy to deal with her, which left the baby of the family—though she'd been in high school—to head across town after midnight. Jonah had never let her go alone.

There had only been one time Martin had been busy, but that wasn't important, and he'd loaned her Jonah's truck.

"I'm sorry." He sighed. "I'm here to protect you, but I'm also here because there's a chance Fix will show up again. It's where he was running to last night. I'm not going to lie to you, Elise. My team and I are working right now."

"And I'm the job?"

He looked disappointed. "On paper maybe. But you know that's not the truth. You've nearly been hurt twice in as many days. I'm looking for Fix, but there's no way his running into the zoo yesterday was a coincidence. If it was, I'd be seriously surprised.

"Until I know for sure the threat against you

has been resolved, or that it has nothing to do with my case, I'm your shadow."

"And if it has nothing to do with my case?" Elise didn't know that she liked it being called that. A file was too bland to represent her nearly being killed.

"I'll have to turn your protection over to the police, just like the investigation into the bomb and the reporter's death."

She swallowed.

"The initial report said he died early this morning, hours before you were shot at by my mailbox." His voice was low, but full of determination. "That's why I'm here, because for some reason you're wrapped up in this and I'm going to find out why."

Elise's voice came out breathy. "He was murdered?"

Jonah got close. "Nothing is going to happen to you."

She should just leave. Why had she even come back? Elise didn't care about construction, or renovation. She wanted to look after animals, not revamp a zoo that had been run down years ago in a town she hadn't liked when she lived here. And she'd brought her son to this place?

Her breath was coming in gasps. "You need to take Nathan away from here."

Pain filled her chest. It felt like her heart was breaking. She wanted her son with her, but if she was in danger the last thing she wanted was for Nathan to be in a killer's crosshairs.

"Mom—"

She looked up, her gaze filled with Jonah— full grown, and capable of keeping her son safe when she couldn't. "He can't be with me."

"He can go to my mother's."

"No." Nathan's voice was firm.

Jonah glanced at him, so Elise did the same. She saw the confusion warring on his face. "You don't have to go anywhere you don't want. But I need you safe, and right now that isn't wherever I am."

Nathan bit his lip. "I could go back to Jonah's."

Whoever had tried to shoot her that morning might be watching the house. Waiting there for her to come home, and shoot Nathan by accident.

Elise shook her head. "I don't think that's an option now."

"My mother's house is secure. She wants to meet you."

Nathan lifted his chin. "Well, I don't want to meet her."

"Nate—"

"My name is Nathan." Her son sucked in a

breath. "And if you're going to send me to your mom's, then you might as well drop me off in that trailer where my mom grew up so I can be abused like she was."

Elise took a step toward him. Nathan shot her a hard look, and she stopped. He wasn't protecting himself; he was trying to protect her from having to revisit the painful parts of her past.

Nathan turned back to Jonah. "You just want to drop me off so you don't have to worry. Well, you can forget it. I don't want my mom or me anywhere near either of those women." He turned and strode away. Eric Hanning followed, keeping a distance, but Elise was confident the marshal wasn't going to let her son out of his sight.

Jonah stepped in front of Elise, his eyes hard the same way her son's had been. "What on earth did you tell him that my mother did to you? He thinks she's some kind of monster."

Jonah folded his arms. He really wanted to know why Elise had essentially poisoned Nathan against his grandmother. Sure, Bernadette Rivers hadn't always been the easiest person to get along with, but this was excessive.

"He's protecting me." Elise pushed out a full

breath. "It was bad. I didn't embellish. I only told Nathan the truth. He's been the man of the family his whole life, and I've tried not to rely on him, but he's a good kid, Jonah. He'll try to protect me anytime he thinks I'm going to get hurt or upset. It's who he is. And he might not be able to protect me from bullets, but he can keep me from this. It's his way."

Jonah figured a good slice of Nathan's honor had come from his father, and his grandfather. But part of it was also down to Elise. She brought out those feelings in anyone who knew her. Not because she was the victim, or she had been when she was a child. Nathan saw something in her that was worth protecting, the same way Jonah and Martin, and their father, had.

He was proud of the way Elise had raised his nephew. The kid was going to be a noble man who took things in stride, and understood the importance of family.

"Dom told me your mom wants to make amends."

Elise didn't look like she thought too much of that. He could appreciate how it might seem like too little, too late, if his mom had truly been bad enough to make Elise gun-shy to the point she didn't want her or Nathan around Bernadette.

"I know it was bad." Jonah gave her a second. "She told me she got saved recently."

Shock flashed across Elise's features. "She did?"

"I've seen a change in her. It's okay if you want to protect yourself from being hurt again, or more, and if you want to protect Nathan. Maybe not right now, given everything that's going on. But at some point it might be worth giving her the benefit of the doubt."

Jonah didn't know how else to convince her. Elise looked so vulnerable, staring up at him with those huge brown eyes. It was like gazing into a past that had always pulled him in like a magnet. Her presence in his life anchored him the way nothing in his life ever had before.

At once he realized what it was that had been missing for so long. The pain of losing his brother, and Elise at the same time, had left him aimless. He'd walked through the past eighteen years with nothing to center him, no anchor to give him a reason to come home at the end of the day. He'd lived for work, because that was all he'd had. His mom had moved on, finding new love with Dom, while Jonah had only known the yawning expanse of loneliness.

Hailey stepped up beside him, breaking the moment. "I can take Nathan to my dad's place.

It's a full house, but one more won't make a difference and he'll be safe for the time being."

Jonah waited, allowing Elise to be the one to make the decision. She looked at him, and he nodded. He'd been content to stay out of it, and she'd included him. For the first time since he'd seen her the day before, it felt like maybe they could be on the same team—and the same page.

Elise turned to Hailey. "If it's fine with Nathan, it's fine with me. He's almost an adult. I'm confident he's able to make the decision for himself."

Shelder strode away, shoulders back and head high in her "work" stance.

"So I—"

His phone rang.

"Sorry." What she'd been about to say was going to have to wait. "This ring tone means it's one of my team."

She stepped away, going back to her debris while Jonah answered the call from Parker. "Rivers."

"Fix's personal effects are in the back bedroom of his mom's trailer. We found the girlfriend—who is pregnant, incidentally—also living there. Claims she hasn't seen Fix, but it's obvious he's been there recently."

"And the mom?"

Elise glanced over, but Jonah didn't give away that he was talking about her mother.

Parker said, "Isn't here. Don't know where she is."

Jonah had a few ideas where she might be, although how she was still up to her same old ways all these years later without detrimental effects on her health was anyone's guess. "See if you can find out. I'm guessing cooperation is a long shot, but it's worth a try."

After Jonah hung up, he tried to figure whether Elise would want to know she was going to have a niece or nephew soon—assuming the girlfriend's baby was Fix's. Who knew?

"What is it?"

He must be tired if he was off his game enough that he was giving his thoughts away with his expression. He needed to be able to school his features better. Not to deceive Elise, but because his job required it. If he started slipping around Elise, it would start happening when it really counted.

Jonah rubbed his hand across his side.

"You keep doing that. Is something wrong with your stomach?"

"I was shot."

Elise gasped, covering her mouth with her hand.

"It was a few weeks ago, during the flood.

It's mostly healed, but it still hurts. If I've been moving a lot, or if it's been a long day."

"Do you want to sit?"

Jonah looked around at the sodden pieces of wood, drywall and bent enclosures. "No, I don't want to sit."

Elise's face morphed into disappointment. "I'm only trying to help."

It wasn't help; it was care. Something Jonah didn't exactly know how to accept. He hadn't had much experience with people caring for him. When he was sick, he just opened a can of soup and microwaved it. When he was better, he went back to work. That was it.

Elise was looking at him with entirely too much heart in her eyes. It was going to make him say something he shouldn't, or admit too much.

"Fix's girlfriend is pregnant."

Elise blinked and her eyes widened. "She is?" She hesitated. "Who is it? Do I know her?"

"Janessa Franks." Jonah didn't remember her from school, but Elise might.

"Huh." Elise glanced aside, like she was trying to remember. "Maybe when I see her face I'll recognize her."

"You're going to see her?"

"Why wouldn't I?"

Jonah shrugged with his mouth. "Maybe

because she's living in one of the places you said you were never going to go."

"I'm not going to exclude her from my life. She might need something."

"You don't even know this woman."

"Why are you questioning that I would help her? She's family."

Jonah huffed out a breath. She was the same way with animals, unrelentingly compassionate even when she'd been bitten. Repeatedly. The woman just wasn't going to quit giving until it killed her.

"Same old Jonah." Elise laughed. "You just can't share your real feelings, can you?"

"Who says I'm not sharing them? Maybe you're just looking for the wrong thing."

She frowned. "What are you saying?"

Jonah shrugged. "Never mind."

If she wasn't going to try and figure it out, then it wasn't worth explaining and making a complete fool of himself.

"Let's just get some of this done."

He turned in time to see a dark-dressed figure sprint between the remainder of two buildings. A man.

"Stay here." Jonah ran after him.

NINE

Jonah's boots pounded the concrete and Elise watched him follow the dark figure until he was out of sight. Stay here? That was all she was supposed to do? She glanced around, surveying the run-down zoo with the eyes of someone who'd had a harrowing two days. And it wasn't over.

She shivered, her gaze darting from shadow to shadow without stopping as she turned in a circle. Silver eyes flashed with the reflection of the setting sun, and Shera padded into view. Elise stepped, slow and careful, toward her. She crouched. Would the old tiger even recognize her scent?

The tiger's footfalls were hesitant, as though she knew there were hidden obstacles everywhere that her blind eyes couldn't see. Elise let her breath out slowly. Shera tilted her head and then walked closer.

Elise kept her voice low. "I should have got

the tranquilizer from my backpack." The animal didn't know she was planning to subdue it. "I only wanted to say hi."

The tiger stopped arm's reach away from Elise.

"I don't have any food. You look hungry." Which, with a tiger, was never good. "I feel bad for the local wildlife, or whatever else you've been snacking on."

The tiger waited. Elise looked down one side and then moved right without stepping to look down the tiger's other flank. "You seem okay. I don't see anything that needs treating, but you're probably cold. How about I—"

Shera shifted, her sightless gaze moving to peer over Elise's shoulder. The tiger was off and running before she could even react. Elise turned to scold Jonah for scaring her away, but it was Fix who stepped into view.

Her brother had aged far more than the almost twenty years since she'd seen him. He'd been lanky but healthy the last time she'd seen him. Now he was thin, too thin. His hair hung in clumps, covering the top of his ears and his forehead under the threadbare knit cap on his head. His old army jacket was frayed and hung loosely over dirty jeans and scuffed boots.

Elise had hardly lived the high life as a single mom struggling in a small sanctuary that existed on donations, but she knew then she'd fared better than her brother.

"Fix."

He kept walking until he was right in front of her. Elise backed up a step, intimidated by his stance. She saw his eyes flare at her retreat, and decided she'd better hold her ground.

"Fix."

Jonah was off chasing him. What was he going to do when he found them? Her brother needed to go, but she wanted time with him, too. What was she supposed to do?

Her brother looked her up and down. "I heard you were hurt, but you look like you're doing okay."

Elise's side was bruised from the attack, but he probably didn't want the whole story. He looked ready to get out of there. "Why are you in so much trouble? The marshals are after you."

Fix glanced around. "Got in deep with some guys. They're into everything. First I was doing odd jobs because I need the money. Janessa found out she was pregnant, so I needed more. Doctors' appointments and vitamins and all that stuff." He sniffed. "Now they're trying to get me on some stupid charge that was overblown by the police."

Elise doubted it was a mistake if Fix's darting eyes and evasive twitching were anything to go by. If it was the police who were chasing him, then maybe. For Jonah and his team of marshals to be involved meant it was a big deal. Fix had to have skipped a court appearance or be evading arrest to be on the run from a fugitive-apprehension task force like the one Jonah ran—or so Hailey had explained to her when she told Elise what their team did.

Fix's mouth moved from a pressed line to curl up the way it did when he wasn't impressed. "I see you don't believe me. Don't much care, though. I heard you were all tight with Marshal Rivers. Yeah, just like old times, right?"

Elise stood her ground. "Does Janessa need anything? I can help." She wasn't going to tell him about Nathan. Not when she wasn't even certain she was safe around her brother. Her own flesh and blood.

God, why did You give me a family that barely tolerated me when things were good?

"We don't need your charity. You're probably raking it in, or getting close to Rivers again, working on your big payout, huh?"

"It's not like that. It never was." Elise sighed. "You knew that then. I don't know why all of a sudden you'd think that now."

"I know you always thought you were better than us. Trailing after those rich boys like hundred-dollar bills would fall out of their pockets. Thinking you're better than where you came from."

"I am better than where I came from. And so are you. For that matter, so is Mom. She just never cared to do more than drink away her life."

"You betrayed her. You spat on our family even before you married Martin, then you moved in to that mansion so you could better pretend to be one of them." Fix's eyes flashed. "Why couldn't you just stay away? Now the feds are breathing down Mom's neck. Janessa is stressed out, and it's not good for the baby."

"I never meant for her to get upset. I didn't tell Jonah to send his people to the trailer. None of this has anything to do with me." She lifted her arms and then let them drop back to her sides. "If anything, this is about you evading capture."

First Jonah, and now her brother. Why did everyone seem to think she was the cause of this? Even the newspaper reporter thought she had something to do with exotic animal trading, as though she would stoop to something that despicable. It was unthinkable. People who traded helpless animals like that were the worst kind of humans, deliberately harming—not

only physically, but more often emotionally—
a living being God had created.

Elise hated the fact someone had been doing
that at the zoo she'd so loved as a child. She'd
spent hours taking care of the animals, working alongside the zookeeper who'd been killed
during the flood.

She knew he'd had enough time to trans-
fer the larger animals and ones that required
constant care out of town when the evacuation
order had been given. The handful of ones that
required only regular care were sent to Sienna's ranch.

So why had he gone back to an empty zoo?
Had it been for more nefarious purposes?

The image of Zane Ford, wearing that fedora
he'd never taken off, desperately trying to save
what he could of the zoo and being swallowed
up by a rush of floodwaters, flew across her
mind. What he must have been through, just to
save the thing he loved most in the world.Elise
could imagine the man going out like that. A
hero to the end.

Elise turned back to Fix. "Jonah will be back
any minute. He ran after you." She didn't want
him to escape justice. Not if he was going to
end up hurting someone. But she also didn't
want to be exactly what he thought she was—
the one who betrayed her family.

Elise was stuck in the middle. Fix going to jail was right, but she didn't have to like it.

"It's just like you to stick up for him." He shoved her then. Elise lifted her arms, bracing herself even though she had no idea what was coming. Fix's body twisted with his shoulder, and his fist swung toward her face.

Jonah saw the punch coming seconds before Fix moved. He ducked out from behind the wall and ran at Elise's brother. Before Fix's fist could make contact with her, Jonah slammed into the man he'd been chasing for weeks.

Fix rolled, the momentum taking both him and Jonah over rocks and other sharp debris that cut into Jonah's shoulders and back. But they didn't stop. Not until Jonah had the hold on Fix that he wanted. Finally he had the man pinned, arms behind his back while Jonah pulled cuffs from his back pocket. When Fix was secured, Jonah lifted him to sit on the ground, legs outstretched in front of him.

Jonah set one hand on his gun, and said, "Talk."

He'd already sent a text to his team, when he first doubled back and saw Fix approach Elise and the tiger. He'd waited to see what the man would reveal to his sister, but stepped in the minute it escalated to violence. The rest of his people should be there within ten minutes.

Fix hunched his shoulders and looked up, his flat gaze on Jonah as though daring him to do something in front of Elise that would make her hate both of them. If Fix thought Jonah wasn't entirely able to push aside his personal feelings, then the man had a lot to learn about how he operated as a US marshal.

Jonah stared back, his look equally as flat as Fix's. "I want to know who you're working with."

"You think I'm just going to tell you? Just like that?"

"I think you will if you want to make sure your family is kept safe while you're in jail. If you're wrapped up in what I think you are, this isn't just about you." Jonah paused. "So tell me what you know about exotic animal trading."

Fix snorted. "Stupid reporter. Got what he deserved, didn't he?"

"Did you kill him?"

Elise gasped, but despite asking the question, Jonah didn't actually think Fix had done the job. It was way too professional for that. Fix wasn't more than an opportunist looking for a quick dollar.

"I didn't kill him. Don't you dare put that on me. I was miles away."

"I suppose you had an alibi, too?"

Fix sniffed. "I could get one."

He probably could. The man knew enough people he could pay to swear under oath that Fix was elsewhere at the time of the murder. Fix had likely been up to something else at the time. But what?

"Tell me what you know about the reporter's article."

When Fix didn't say anything, Elise stepped forward. "Was the zoo a holdover for animals being illegally bought and sold?" Her voice was high and tight, with an edge of emotion she only just had a rein on.

Fix looked up at her. Not the look one would expect from an older brother only recently reunited with his sister. But then, Fix had never thought much of little Elise. She'd adored him, and he'd brushed off her affection at best.

He turned to Jonah. "I'm not giving you his name."

"Because you don't know, or because it's your only leverage?"

"I want a deal."

Of course he did. Everyone wanted to make a bargain when they had nothing left. No criminal he'd ever met was willing to accept the consequences of their actions. They only ever wanted to escape justice.

"Just tell me about the zoo right now."

Fix worked his jaw from side to side. "The reporter died because he knew too much. Shouldn't have dipped his nose in if he couldn't protect himself, should he?"

"If you're worried the same will happen to you, being in custody comes with our protection."

"That's exactly why you're not taking me in." Fix's mouth pressed into a tight line. "I can't afford to be on paper where he'll get to me. Why do you think the bomb in the office exploded all the evidence? It's why I was coming here."

"Not because you heard your sister was back in town, or because you worried someone would get hurt." Jonah figured Fix had been heading there to get the evidence for himself before it was destroyed so he'd actually have concrete leverage when the time came.

"I'm dead if I can't give him a reason to keep me alive."

Elise whispered, "I can't believe you'd be a part of this."

"I needed the money." Fix turned his hard stare to his sister. "And now I'm dead because of it."

Jonah said, "Why is he doing this?"

"Wrapping things up." Fix glanced around, like the man he was talking about might be listening. "Starting fresh somewhere else, doesn't want to leave lose ends."

Elise stepped in front of Jonah. "And you don't care that he's trying to kill me, too?"

Jonah was glad she didn't mention Nathan. He didn't want Fix to get any ideas about using his nephew in all this.

"Why would I?" Fix shrugged, belligerence clear on his face. "It's not like you cared at all about us while you were living the high life."

Parker, Ames and Hanning made their approach, surrounding them. When Parker reached Elise, Jonah nodded without taking his gaze from Fix.

"Why don't we step over here?" Parker's words weren't a question. He held Elise's elbow as he led her away from her brother.

Every criminal they chased was considered a flight risk, and Fix was no exception. But the opportunity to get to the bottom of this couldn't be ignored. If they took Fix into custody, then Elise would still be in danger, and her brother would likely shut down and desist giving them any more intel. Fix knew who was behind this, he just didn't want to give it up.

But if Jonah could get on the inside, he had a chance to catch the man for himself and end the danger to Elise.

He studied Fix, wondering just how connected the man was. Between the person at the root of the illegal animal trading and the person who had killed the reporter and shot at Elise, Jonah figured there were at least two involved. Fix would make the third, an expendable extra at best, given that he had little to no skills to speak of aside from time and what came out of his mouth. Fix had always been able to talk his way out of trouble—it was why his mom was so sweet on him, at the expense of Elise.

Fix's eyes narrowed. Jonah didn't much care if he didn't like the look on his face. "You have this guy's number?"

Fix said, "Supposed to do a job for him soon."

Jonah figured there wasn't a lot of time if the illegal animal trader was wrapping up his operation and moving it elsewhere. Jonah needed to beat this guy to the trigger if he was going to keep Elise—and Nathan—safe. And if he secured Fix's cooperation now, he would still be able to ensure justice for the crimes Fix had committed later.

The fact that the job had become personal wasn't lost on him. Jonah could be objective, but that was going to go out the window fast, and everyone on his team knew it. If he didn't finish this, the window of opportunity would close.

The trader would move on to the next place never to be found, and Elise would be dead.

Jonah hauled Fix to his feet. "I want an introduction."

Going undercover wasn't completely unorthodox in his line of work, though it wasn't usually necessary. He was going to have to fill out a whole load of paperwork to justify it, but Jonah found he didn't much care about that.

Fix's eyes widened. "You want…what?"

"From now on, I'm your new best friend."

TEN

Elise stood back while Jonah ordered the tall one, Parker, and the mouthy one, Ames, to stay on Fix. They were letting him go?

Parker nodded, like this was business as usual. "I'll put a bug on him, and we'll stick close, but out of sight. We don't want the trader to spot us and then run."

Jonah said, "Great."

The two marshals walked Fix away from her, something that didn't bother Elise much. It hadn't exactly been a happy reunion with her brother. He was going to jail, and she was going to try not to get killed.

Eric stepped close to Jonah. "I'm going to head to Hailey's and check on Nathan. Make sure they're all doing okay."

Jonah nodded.

He wandered over to Elise. Apparently they didn't have anywhere to be, the way everyone else seemed to. His lips tilted up in a smile.

"He just wants to tell his girls good-night. Hailey lives with her dad, and her daughter—she's thirteen—already calls Eric 'dad.' She didn't want to wait for the wedding."

Elise smiled. "That's cute." She looked around, suddenly overwhelmed by all the work there was. But she didn't have to do it tonight. The mayor knew it would take weeks to get things back to normal, much like the rest of the town's slow recovery after the flood.

"Do you want me to go over things with you? Explain what's happening with Fix?"

Elise shrugged. She grabbed her notebook and meandered around debris to her discarded backpack.

"We'll keep a close eye on him for now, let him go about his business while we're watching. Parker and Ames will be able to track him, and if Fix has a phone they'll put a trace on it. We'll be able to hear when he gets a call, and if it's the animal trader, then we'll be able to run a voice analysis."

She turned to him and Jonah continued. "I've explained to Fix what we want. For him to set a meeting, and I'll join him as his 'partner.' We'll go to see the trader wherever Fix is supposed to meet up with the man, and I'll find out who it is. It's a sting operation, but it's also the only way I'm going to get close enough to this guy to find out who it is and be able to catch him in the act so we can arrest him."

She measured his words. The buzz of doing his job and enjoying it was there, but also something else. "I don't need you to justify it to me. Fix doesn't want me in his life."

"I'm not going to let him hurt you."

If she was honest, it was too late for that. Jonah understood a need for physical safety, but he had no jurisdiction over Fix's ability to bruise her emotionally. He never had.

That was just something Elise had to live with, and deal with, considering the fact Fix would always be her brother.

"It's been years." She glanced at the trees, shadowed in the evening darkness. "I thought they couldn't hurt me because I was gone, like that would keep me from heartache. Nathan filled a lot of corners, a lot of spaces in my heart that were just…bare. I thought that would be enough, but my heart refuses to quit recognizing Fix, and my mother, as family."

She shook her head. "No matter what they do, or how they are, they shouldn't have the ability to bruise me like this. They don't care, so why should I?"

"When you left, how did you know you were supposed to go?" He hesitated a second. "I know you had a job offer, but you could've stayed and worked here at the zoo. How did you know you were making the right decision for you, and then for Nathan?"

He looked so unsure, Elise wanted to reach out and comfort him. Would Jonah accept that, when he was still in his "work" mode? They were alone, but it wasn't like they were close now.

She thought about his question. "I didn't know about Nathan until after I was in Idaho. But God gave me peace about it. Actually the where didn't matter too much. But I didn't want to come home. I wanted a new place. I just knew that wherever I was, and whatever I was doing, that God would take care of me and Nathan. He wasn't going to leave us hanging."

"God?"

"First I had to make peace with Him, it's contingent on that. Then He can give you His peace." She locked eyes with him. "He's never let me down. Not once."

A darkness flickered in his eyes, like he'd taken on something she hadn't intended to say. She hadn't been thinking about her and Jonah. God was on a different plane. He didn't shift and change the way people did, but it was true that nearly everyone in her life had let her down.

Jonah knew that sad truth. But he also

needed to know she hadn't spent years wallowing. She'd rested in God's gifts of joy and peace, and raised her son. She'd found her strength in God.

He gifted her a small smile. "I don't think I've had any peace at all since my dad died."

She nodded. It had been hard for her, too. Though not as hard as it was for him, Martin or Bernadette. Losing Nathan Senior had been a blow. "You have to find it for yourself. You can't piggyback off someone else's faith. You have to make peace with God on your own."

Elise figured if explaining this to Jonah, planting that seed for God to grow his faith, was the only reason she'd come home, she was fine with it. *Thank you, Lord.* She'd wondered a lot over the years where Jonah was, how his walk with the Lord was. Now she knew. And while it saddened her that he'd missed so many years of being in fellowship with God, she also knew it was never too late to turn around.

And while she could push him to make a decision now, Jonah was the kind of man who had to think through all the angles before he made a choice. It was why his leaving to join the marines bothered her so much. Obviously he'd thought long about it before leaving. He just hadn't talked it over with her.

His head titled to the side. "What is it?"

Elise didn't think. She just blurted it out. "Why did you leave?"

Did she really want him to answer that question? Elise was in no way ready for the truth about how strong his feelings for her had been back then. She'd been fifteen, much too young for what—only a few years later—would have been perfectly acceptable.

The only thing for him to do was put space between them. Their friendship had been strong enough it would have survived the years and the distance. Or so he'd thought.

"Are you going to tell me why you married my brother of all people?"

Jonah loved Martin, but his brother had been the party one. How he'd managed to convince Elise to marry him was anyone's guess. She needed someone steady, not the guy who did things on a whim.

Jonah followed her as she strode, head high, in the direction of his truck. Apparently they weren't going to talk about that now. Eventually they'd have to lay it all out, but it could come later. He was willing to let her have time now. He'd waited long enough already. He would get his answers, though. It was too important to just let it go. Again.

Or maybe he didn't want to know. If he'd

known when he left that she wasn't going to
wait for him, he'd probably have stayed. But
then he'd have had to see her every day knowing she didn't feel the same way he felt. He'd
rather undergo severe torture than have to face
that.

What if she didn't feel the way he did?

Jonah blew out a breath and started the engine, not looking at Elise lest he see it written
there on her face.

Her words about peace with God were still
with him. Maybe that was what he needed. He
barely even knew why he'd voiced the question.
Usually he didn't suffer attacks of doubt over
operational decisions. That had never happened
until she showed up.

The truth was, the cost had reached stag-
gering proportions. There was no way he was
going to allow himself to be beaten. Not this
time. If Elise and Nathan's presence here meant
he had to double back and rethink everything,
that was fine. So long as they were still moving somehow.

As much as he could, Jonah was going to
keep them safe. It was the variables that worried him so much, those thousand things he had
absolutely no control over.

Whether Elise reciprocated or not, Jonah still
cared about her. He cared for his nephew, even

though he barely knew the teen. They were his family, and they always had been even though he'd been an idiot not to track Elise down for himself. He'd needed her in his life.

Plain and simple.

He'd just needed her.

There was something about Elise that brought him to his knees. It was like being cracked open and laid bare for everyone in the world to see. The scariest thing in the world, and yet the one thing he didn't think he could live without. The years had proven that, if nothing else.

And she'd brought something else with her that she hadn't possessed before. Elise now had a wisdom that drew him in and made him believe there might be a God who would never let him fall. Despite the fact his father and brother had died. Despite the fact she'd left.

Could God still really be good, even through all that?

"You always were sort of broody, but this is ridiculous."

Jonah glanced at her. "I'm not the only one not speaking."

"Great. Now we're going to argue about who started it."

"No, we're not, Lise. We're not ready to go there yet, and that's fine. We have time."

"I hope so." Her words were soft.

So soft, Jonah reached over and covered her hand with his. He gave it a gentle squeeze and then let go.

Out of the corner of his eye, she glanced at him again. "Who are you?"

Jonah looked over then. He shrugged.

"I think the Jonah I knew got lost over the years, because once in a while there's this flash that feels familiar, but you're so different from the guy I knew. If you're going to be in mine and Nathan's lives like you want, then we're going to have to get to know each other from the beginning again."

"We still have things to talk about."

"I'm not saying we shouldn't do that. Eventually. We can't bury it, but we also can't think we know each other."

Jonah said, "You know me."

She shook her head. "Maybe it's been too long. Maybe I don't anymore, as much as I might want to."

Jonah pressed his lips together, trying to decide if he was okay with what she'd said. Part of him wanted to rail against it. They'd always known each other. Their friendship had been effortless. The years had been long, but still— how could they be strangers? The connection was as strong as it always had been. He'd known that the first minute he saw her again.

Jonah made the right turn, taking the highway back to his house. Headlights glared, coming toward them.

At the last second he wondered that they weren't moving back in their lane. The vehicle was swerving into his, coming at his car faster than he might be able to react. A giant black truck, the front bumper level with Jonah's window.

Elise gripped the dash, bracing herself. They were going fast, but he was going to have to risk it.

Jonah held his foot down on the gas pedal, picking up speed until the last second. Elise screamed. He pulled his foot from the gas and reached with his left hand across the steering wheel, swung the wheel in one hard motion and pulled up the hand brake at the same time.

Elise screamed through the entire turn. When they started to straighten, to face the way they'd been coming, Jonah released his grip on the steering wheel, letting it slide through his fingers so they could straighten fully. He released the hand brake, changed down to second gear and hit the gas. When they got up to speed, he put it back in drive.

Elise sucked in a breath. "You're going to kill us! What *was* that?"

"A hand-brake turn."

The truck that had been coming at them, determined to crash into them, was now in a ditch on the side of the road, judging by the angle of the lights in his rearview mirror.

As they sped away, Jonah waited. Watched. The brake lights blinked out and the truck roared away in the opposite direction. The driver wasn't hurt, but he was likely going to regroup and try again later.

Elise was gasping. "You think I know you? I don't. You never would have done that."

"I would have if I'd needed to save your life." Jonah selected his phone on the display and waited while it rang in the car's speakers.

"Shelder."

"Keep watch tonight. Someone just tried to run us off the road."

"You guys okay?" Hailey was in work mode. Jonah said, "We're fine."

"We most certainly are *not* fine!" Elise's yell was loud in the cab.

Hailey chuckled. "Alive, aren't you?"

"Barely."

For some reason Elise's reaction made him smile. Maybe she was right, maybe they didn't know each other now. He had the feeling she'd discover plenty of things about him before they were done. Would she react like this for all of them?

"Are you laughing at me?"

Hailey laughed. "I'm hanging up now."

Jonah clicked the phone off on his end, just because he didn't want anyone listening by accident. Or on purpose. "They were going to try and kill us. Or me, and then kidnap you. Would you rather have experienced that, or do what we just did?"

"Neither."

"Face the fact that this is happening, Elise."

"I'm not in denial. But I don't have to like it." She folded her arms. "You scared the life out of me."

Better him than anyone else.

Jonah grabbed her hand again. This time he brought it close to his mouth, touching his lips to the soft skin on the back of her hand. Elise was completely still and silent while he said, "Nothing will happen to you if I can help it."

ELEVEN

Jonah pulled into the underground parking garage that served their whole building, not just the floors that housed the Marshals' downtown offices. His phone beeped, so he checked the email notification.

"Cops will be here in ten minutes."

Elise didn't say anything. Jonah didn't know how he was supposed to relieve her fears. It was good that she was afraid. That respect for the danger she was in would help keep her alive.

Jonah swiped his access card and signed Elise in with the duty receptionist. The office had a few lights on, but most people were home for the night if they weren't out working like his team. Jonah's office was at the end, next to the conference room. He unlocked the door and motioned Elise to his couch.

She sank into the cushions, huddled in the corner and pulled out her phone—the replacement Hailey had given her. Jonah figured she was texting Nathan, but she could just as easily be posting to her social media accounts about how awful a US marshal he was and what a bad job he was doing of protecting her.

Jonah sat behind his desk and cleared his inbox of things he could solve in a second, filing the emails that weren't urgent and would take longer to respond to for Monday morning. Was she simply going to retreat into silence? He'd never seen her so defeated as she was now, finally recognizing the strength of the threat. His confusion lay in the fact that she'd apparently only fully comprehended this at the point she was in danger—when she should be grasping the fact that he could protect her.

It wasn't pride; it was an understanding of the skills he'd been honing half his life. Maybe Elise was right, maybe she was trying to get to know a stranger, even despite their connection. He could only hope all that work was enough to help her, and part of that was her needing to trust him when it counted. If she hesitated and didn't trust him, things could go wrong. Jonah was assuming a lot, counting on his skills. But between that and Elise praying about everything so she had the peace she'd been talking about, they were covered.

Elise took a shaky breath. Jonah looked over without turning his head and saw her wipe under her eye. Jonah locked his computer and went to sit by her. "How's Nathan?"

Some of the tension bled from her posture. "Helping Hailey's father install a new screen door because the puppy Eric bought Hailey's daughter chewed through the old one."

Jonah chuckled.

She glanced at him. "How much did you hear before you tackled Fix?"

"All of it."

She shook her head. "I can't believe he said I betrayed them. Why does he even care what I did? It's like trying to be happy, moving out and finding my own life was wrong."

"But—"

"They suddenly decide to be offended the first time I ever do for myself, because apparently I'm supposed to be one of them until death."

Jonah could actually see how they might feel betrayed by her leaving them behind. People like that, who'd spent Elise's entire life telling her that she'd never make anything of herself or that she would never go anywhere else than their small town, would hate being proven wrong. Her mom and brother were only going to feel good about who and what they were if Elise never rose above exactly where they'd tried to keep her.

She blinked. "You agree with them?"

"I get their point. From where they stand you did betray them."

Jonah met selfish people like that every single day. People who thought nothing of dragging others down with them. People who knowingly hurt those they were supposed to care for. It was a fact of life, but she couldn't see that because she was still under the impression families were supposed to always love each other. But the world didn't usually turn out the way it was "supposed" to.

"I didn't betray them."

"I only said *they* think you did," Jonah said. "Not that you were selfish. If you hadn't left with Nathan, where would you be now?"

She was quiet for a moment. "It's not like I loaded him in the car and drove away. I didn't even know I was pregnant. When I left town I was nothing but a scared kid with one suitcase, enough gas money to get to the sanctuary in Idaho and the promise of a job that had to be better than being here where everything reminded me of Martin."

"You seem like you've taken care of both of you just fine."

"Sure, we lived in a really nice trailer that leaked when it rained." She smiled, but there was no humor there. "It was a perk of the job, the sanctuary owner's dead uncle's trailer he didn't want to put any money in to repairing."

"You had the death benefits, though. That must have seen you through having Nathan and setting up your life. Did you invest any of it, or just use it to support you?"

Elise's brow crinkled enough that dread settled in Jonah's stomach. "What?" She said, "I didn't have any money other than what was in the bank at the time—my last paycheck from the zoo. And the bills for my student loans."

"So you never claimed the death benefits?"

"What are you talking about?"

"The military compensates the family, to help them. It's not a lot, but it should have helped you. Why did you have nothing? Didn't they offer it to you? You were Martin's next of kin. My mom was mine, but he'd have signed his to you in the event he was killed in action."

"Your mom dealt with everything for me. She never said anything to me about money."

"What about Martin's life insurance?"

Elise said, "Do you think if I'd had any insurance that I would have lived in a run-down camping trailer until Nathan was ten? Eventually I saved enough for a two-bedroom apartment, but we certainly never lived the high life with all this cash you think I had."

Jonah shook his head, not quite believing

his mom hadn't made sure Elise had what she needed. He'd have to talk with her, to find out what had happened to the insurance and the military death benefits that should have been Elise's. She hadn't known Elise was pregnant, but still… He couldn't comprehend disliking someone that much that you would tear down the security of her entire future.

"It doesn't matter now." Elise shook her head. "Nathan will have college money. I'll have a place to stay at the zoo, and everything will be fine."

Be that as it may, Jonah wasn't going to deny Elise something that should rightfully have been hers. It wasn't like his mom had needed the money. What had she done with it?

Jonah glanced at his phone, sat on the top of his desk. He could wait until daylight tomorrow, but he was going to be calling his mother and talking with her. Or he could wait until this all blew over and Elise wasn't in danger anymore.

Either way, he'd find out what happened.

Elise's head was still reeling from what Fix had said. And now, on top of that, Jonah had thought all these years that she had taken the money from Martin's death to fund her new life.

She couldn't believe he'd think she was so

callous as to have simply taken the money and left. He'd known her better than that.

Money was important, but it wasn't the most important thing.

When she was growing up, it had seemed like every single person around her thought money was the source of a person's value. Even the Rivers brothers, though maybe it was just part of how they were raised.

It had taken her years to come to the place where she'd no longer been hurt by one careless comment or other, which they probably hadn't meant anything by anyway. They were no more responsible for their upbringing than she'd been for hers.

She'd tried to leave the past in the past, and Nathan had been her fresh start. God had taken the stains of the life she'd left here. He'd allowed her to forgive her family and the town who'd seen her as one of them.

She knew she was going to be safe now. God would take care of her and Nathan, no matter what. He always had, even through all the lean and lonely years.

The fact was, if she'd had all that money Jonah thought she should have had, her life might have been easier. But she never would have learned the lesson God had wanted her to learn—the lesson of fully trusting in Him. Not just for some things, but for everything.

The door popped open and the marshal who'd signed her in stuck his head in. "Two detectives are here to see you."

Elise waited while Jonah shook their hands. The first cop was the older man who'd interviewed her at Jonah's house—William Manners—and the other had been there, too, his partner. Though they acted casual enough, their eyes were anything but.

Detective Manners nodded. "Ms. Tanner."

She gave him a small wave. "Hi."

"I hear you identified the reporter for some of our officers."

"Yes, though it doesn't seem like it did any good. Not since he was found dead."

The cop shook his head, the honesty plain on his face. "You didn't start any of this. And for the record, I don't like when good people take on board guilt that isn't theirs to carry."

"Uh, okay."

Jonah laughed. "Leave the lecture for the next candidate, yeah, Bill?"

The detective huffed what was probably supposed to have been a laugh. "Can't help the way I feel." He glanced at Elise. "I've been a cop a lot of years. This one—" He pointed to Jonah. "He'll take care of you, and then some."

Elise nodded. "I know that."

Jonah might scare her, but it was obvious he knew what he was doing. If he'd taken an interest in her safety, who was she to turn down his help?

Jonah told them all about the car trying to crash into them, and the evasive maneuver he'd pulled. He looked jazzed, like this was a race and he'd been triumphant. When the officer had finished making notes about the make and model Elise hadn't even noticed, but apparently Jonah had, Jonah said, "What's the latest?"

Jonah's stance was all business. A man of authority used to commanding his team and infinitely comfortable in his own skin. Had she ever felt that confident about herself?

The cop gave her a wink and sat in one of Jonah's chairs. His partner, who was younger and reminded her of Nathan, leaned against the wall.

The older cop settled himself. "Couple of beat cops over on Elm found a trash can on fire in a back alley. They managed to salvage a stack of papers that hadn't burned yet along with the reporter's computer."

"Anything usable on it?"

Manners nodded in answer to Jonah's question. "Hard drive wasn't all the way destroyed, so our techs are uploading, or downloading, or whatever it is with those things. They'll let us know what's on it as soon as they know. I told them to put a rush on it, but everything they have is priority."

"Did you get anything from the papers?"

"It looks like our reporter was making notes the old-fashioned way. And he seemed to think there was some significance to the zookeeper's body never being found after the flood."

Elise said, "Didn't a few people go missing?"

"Sure, but most of those were found in other states, trying to start over. Or their bodies were discovered, eventually."

"But not Zane?"

The cop shook his head. "Never. No sightings of him, and no body."

"What does that mean?"

Jonah said, "It could mean he's not dead."

Detective Manners shrugged. "I doubt it means much, but we're going to look. Not sure where else there is to check, but we'll do it. The zookeeper never had the skills to kill the reporter the way it was done."

"That doesn't mean he's not ultimately responsible." Jonah perched on the edge of his desk. "He could be working with another person."

Elise tried to imagine Zane Ford hurting anyone, or even collaborating to do so. "There's no way. He took care of animals, he wouldn't hurt them. Not to mention, if he was still alive, then someone would have seen him."

Detective Manners nodded. "That's where I'm leaning."

Elise looked at the younger cop to see if he agreed, but the guy was doing something on his cell phone. Apparently he had business to take care of, or he was late for a date or something. It was past eleven at night, and despite sleeping in that morning, Elise was exhausted. And her pain meds were wearing off.

She shifted on the couch, trying to find a more comfortable way to sit that wasn't lying flat, which was what she wanted to do. When nothing was better, and every angle hurt her ribs, Elise sighed.

Jonah was studying her. The cop cleared his throat, which made the other cop look up from his phone screen. Jonah turned to Detective Manners and said, "You keep working your theory. My guys will tackle Zane Ford."

"You think he's alive?" Elise felt her eyebrows rise. "Did Fix tell you something which makes you think that, or are you guessing?"

"Cops don't guess, Elise. We use our best judgment and we find evidence."

"I just can't believe Zane Ford would let people think he was dead all this time."

Jonah's gray eyes darkened. "Maybe you didn't know him as well as you thought you did."

"He ran a zoo. He didn't know how to plant bombs and shoot people."

She might not have been best friends with the man, but she'd respected his work for as long as she'd known him.

The cop nodded. "She's got a point."

"Be that as it may, I'm not going to leave any loose ends."

The younger cop looked up, probably noting the tone of Jonah's raised voice. Still, he didn't look impressed by Jonah's determination.

Detective Manners stood. "If that's all, we'll take our leave."

Jonah nodded, and they both said goodbye to the cops. When they were gone, he turned to her. "Want to get out of here?"

"Sure. I can stay with Hailey if you need to be up early. She said it was fine."

Jonah didn't say anything for a moment. "Is that what you want?"

She eyed him while they walked to the elevator. Why did he look so disappointed? He wanted to focus, find the killer. Right? "It would be nice to be near Nathan, but he probably doesn't want me coddling him in front of other people. And he's texting me updates pretty regularly. He'll be okay with two marshals close by."

She took a breath, waiting to see if he'd accept her offer of company. His guest room bed was more comfy than anywhere she'd slept in years.

They stepped out of the elevator in the parking garage. The whole place was dark and cold. The clack of their shoes echoed off the concrete floor as they walked.

Elise glanced around, then at Jonah. She tried to smile, to show him she wasn't scared. When he reached for her hand she figured it hadn't worked. Jonah's warm palm touched hers, and his fingers folded around hers. Elise wanted to stop. To just breathe in the sensation of having a man hold her hand. It had been a long, long time.

He paused at her door. "If you'd like to stay in my guest room again…"

Elise smiled. "I'll make dinner, if you do the dishes."

"Deal." He let go when she got in the car.

He pulled out onto the street, and Jonah's foot let off the brake, his eyes on a vehicle across the street. "That's the same black truck that nearly ran into us."

TWELVE

Jonah pulled out, despite the urge to drive straight over and give the guy a talking-to for nearly running them off the road earlier. It was the same truck—no plate on the front and it'd been lifted for off-roading. Jonah beat back the urge to confront the guy, knowing he would've had Elise not been in the car. Bringing her to the killer wasn't a good idea, no matter how many skills he had. He needed a way to end this that didn't put her in danger.

Running away and living to fight another day grated against his marine sensibilities, but he was getting too old for all that, anyway. Instead he pulled out his phone and called the office, explaining what was happening even as the car pulled out onto the street behind them.

The duty marshal said, "Beta team is running the operation on Franchez tonight."

Of course they were. Which meant that team and their backups were all busy. While Jonah's team was busy protecting Nathan and watching Fix.

"You want me put a call in to local uniforms?"

Jonah had wanted his team to tail the killer, the ordered way they'd done countless times, chasing one fugitive or another. Explaining what he wanted to the police would take too long.

"I'll take care of it from here." Even if it meant he had no chance of pulling the guy over and arresting him all by himself. The cops would have to take care of that part. "Tell them we spotted the car."

Officers would respond, but they would use the necessary caution. The be-on-the-lookout order he'd issued earlier included the fact that the suspect was likely armed and dangerous.

"Got it."

Jonah hung up.

Elise glanced out the back window. "What are we going to do?"

"We have no backup, but cops will be here soon. I wanted my team to tail him, to hang back so we can catch him. Or follow him home if he breaks off."

"Is he going to run us off the road again? Because if you do that turn with your parking brake again, I'm likely to lose my lunch."

"So noted." He smiled, his attention on the

rearview where the truck was matching pace with them. Was the shooter going to make a move, or follow them home? "Seems like I recall Martin being the one with the nervous stomach, not you."

She laughed. "He did like to complain when I brought him injured animals."

"Or the time that bunny had babies." Jonah was pretty sure it had been a bunny.

"Flopsy!" Elise laughed again. "I forgot all about her. Martin really didn't like that, but I cleaned up his bathroom after even if it did make me miss my curfew. Your mom never even knew. Your housekeeper looked funny at me, though. She probably found a little pile of rabbit droppings under something."

Jonah smiled. The housekeeper they'd had back then never liked mess of any kind. She never said anything, though. But she didn't need to, considering how adept she'd been at glaring.

"I know you're just trying to distract me so I don't freak out." Elise looked back again. "He's still there. Can we do something?"

"Like goad him into losing his cool?"

She shrugged.

Jonah said, "Depends how much of a plan he has. Some people have a short fuse. Then again, I knew this one guy in the army, never got flustered. Not ever. He held it in so well, I saw him pass out once, but he never lost his cool."

The truck got closer. Jonah braced for impact, but it never came.

He sped up. The truck matched his speed.

He slowed down, and the truck did the same.

Minutes later they were out of the busy part of town on the unlit highway.

The closer they got to his house, the more certain Jonah was that the driver was waiting for a particular spot.

And he knew exactly which one it was going to be.

"He's closer now."

Jonah gritted his teeth. "There's a sharp turn coming up."

"So do that thing." Elise's voice was desperate.

Jonah squeezed her knee, fast, then gripped the wheel with both hands again. "He'll be expecting that. He'll just ram us and run us off the edge, anyway."

"A cliff?"

"No, into the river." Ending up in ice-cold water would be a bad end to an all-around bad day. "All we have to do is stay on the road."

But while his SUV was heavy, the other vehicle was more like a tank. Or a brick that sank. If the truck slammed them, they would go over.

"Pray the police get here soon."

Fifty feet from the turn Jonah hit the brakes, halting them in an emergency stop. When the truck slammed into the back of them, Jonah pulled up the hand brake, praying his SUV was heavy enough to at least slow down the truck.

Tires screeched on the asphalt, drowned by Elise's scream.

Police lights flashed in his side mirror, still a mile away.

The truck pushed against the back of his car, grinding the bumper, forcing them down the road. But they were still twenty feet from the edge.

The other driver backed off, probably because of the lights and sirens filling his rearview. The truck swung to the left side and pulled alongside Jonah's car.

Before he even registered the machine gun, Jonah yelled, "Get down!"

Elise ducked. He slid into reverse as the gun fired. Bullet after bullet thumped into the car as they shot backward. The window beside Jonah shattered. He drew his gun, flipped off the safety and fired two shots out the broken window as the truck sped away.

Jonah hit the brakes just as a cop car stopped beside him, and another cruiser took off in pursuit.

Jonah exhaled. "He's mad."

Elise looked at him. Her face pale, her breath coming fast. "Ya think?"

"No, I mean the driver. That wasn't a solid kill plan, not like at the mailbox. I bested him earlier with the hand-brake turn. I made him mad."

Elise's mouth curved in the facsimile of a smile that sort of scared him. "Maybe you should think about that before you pull one of those stunt moves again. I'm not sure my heart can take it."

Detective Manners leaned down so his face was level with the broken-out window. "How are you folks doing?"

Jonah turned to him. "Reminiscing about your traffic-stop days?"

"You could say that." He cracked the door. "Turn your legs out. I want a look at your head."

"His head?" Elise got out her side and he heard her steps as she rounded the car. "What's wrong with Jonah's—" She gasped.

"I'm guessing it looks bad." He deliberately smiled at Elise, but that made his face sting.

She swallowed. "You have cuts all down the side of your face."

The younger detective came to stand behind Elise. "Ambulance is on its way."

"And the truck?"

Elise scoffed at Jonah's question. "You

don't need to worry about that right now." She crouched beside him, her fingers twitching like she wanted to touch his head. When was the last time anyone had offered him sympathy like that?

Jonah smiled.

Detective Manners rocked heel to toe and chuckled.

Elise glared at him. "None of this is funny."

Jonah was still smiling. "I know, darlin'."

Elise snorted, the way she always did when he used his cowboy voice. She would know he was okay, however bad it looked. And his face stung something fierce. Jonah pushed out a breath, feeling like an invalid sitting in the car when everyone else was out.

Jonah braced his hand on the door and started to climb out.

Elise's hands were there immediately. "No, no. Stay in the car. You should wait to get checked out. You look pale."

"Bad lighting." He settled back down, but she didn't take her hands away. She smoothed them up his arms to his shoulders, turning his chin to survey the damage. Her face was close enough that if he leaned in he could kiss her.

Jonah had been about to kiss her. Then the ambulance had shown up, and she'd had to back

up so they had room to wipe the blood from
Jonah's face and check that there wasn't glass
in any of the cuts. There hadn't been, thankfully, and none had been so deep they needed
stitches—just those butterfly bandages. The
worst thing was a possible infection from the
dirty glass.

Her hair wet, Elise settled on Jonah's couch
in her own clothes. Never in her life had she
been so appreciative of her own worn-in paja-
mas and her comfy sweater that hung past her
hips. The police had actually released her belongings back to her.

She sighed, eyes closed, probably smiling
like a goofball.

Sure, they'd almost been run off the road.
Again. But after that Jonah had been about to
kiss her.

She was sure.

And it was the whole reason she was cur-
rently acting like her teenage self, massively
crushing on the boy who only thought of her
as "little Elise."

Good thing no one was in the room except
Sam. The dog sat at the opposite end of the
couch, his eyes watching the room.

The floorboard creaked. Sam's ears twitched,

but he didn't move. Elise spied Parker walking down the hall. Maybe he wouldn't see her.

"I can see you."

She glared at the dark hall. "How did you know I was watching you?"

He stepped into the room. "I smelled the dog. Figured you'd be wherever he was."

Parker's wide frame, and the scar she noticed on the side of his neck, added to the menacing figure the shadows tried to hide. He was totally capable of appearing as threatening as he wished. Like Parker could simply step into the darkness and she would never even see him go. Could a man really disappear like that? What if the killer had that kind of training?

Elise shivered.

Parker stepped out into the hall and then back seconds later holding a bundle. He flicked the blanket out and covered her with it.

"Thank you."

He shrugged with his mouth. "No sense in getting a chill."

"It's my hair. It's wet." She even sounded like a teenager with more hormones than brains. Elise shook her head. "What is Jonah doing?"

She hadn't seen him since before she'd gone into the bathroom. He was supposed to be taking a shower, but he should be done by now. Or so she thought.

"He only just went in his bathroom before you came out. He had a bunch of calls to make. Shelder is with your son. Ames and Hanning are watching your brother. Which leaves me with you, so Jonah can get some rest later."

She glanced at the clock. "He was working?" Was she stopping him from doing his job because he was tied up protecting her?

Parker perched on the back of the couch, his upper body turned to face her. "He had to call his boss and give an update. The chief of police. The mayor." Parker grinned. "His mother."

Elise laughed.

"The man doesn't strike me as a mama's boy, but he seems to talk to her a lot."

She asked, "You're not close with your family?"

Parker shrugged one shoulder. Evidently that was all she was going to get out of him.

"I wouldn't describe Jonah as a mama's boy. He argued with her more than he toed the line, but their family was close. Always." She wasn't the only one who'd been grieving when Martin died, especially given it wasn't long after his father's death.

It was why she understood the way Bernadette had acted after Martin's death.

The years had distanced Elise from any sense of betrayal she might have felt over money she should have received. She didn't want to think about that now, not all these years later. As though she was owed, simply because her husband died. It wasn't like she needed the money now—not when her job would cover the essentials, and Nathan's college tuition.

"And then you stepped in, the usurper."

She considered Parker's words. "Yes, you figured that right. I was the epitome of everything they weren't. Martin and Jonah, even their father. Still, none of them ever made me feel unwelcome. And when they were around and their mom was there, they provided a buffer."

She smiled to herself. "This one time, Bernadette was having tea with some hoity society ladies. I'm pretty sure one of them was a senator's wife. One of the baby alligators I'd rescued from the ravine, after someone dumped oil in the water, managed to get out of the bathroom. He walked right into the middle of high tea." She chuckled. "Jonah ran in, scooped the thing up and kept walking, right to the patio door at the end of the sunroom."

Elise laughed aloud. "They were all aghast. His mom said his name, in this total 'mom' voice."

Jonah.

She could still hear it in her head.

"He turned back and said, 'Maybe you should tell them about the alligators, Mother. They need somewhere to live now.'" She laughed. "Like his mom was going to organize a save-the-alligators fund-raiser."

She could see the set of his shoulders in her mind. Jonah had been stepping up for her, trying to find a way she and his mom could establish a common ground. She hadn't even noticed. All she'd seen was the hole when he left.

It struck her then how different her life would have been had she given the family space after Jonah left. Her broken heart could have healed in time.

Martin had insisted they carry on as usual. Then he'd declared his feelings for her in senior year. She'd always loved Martin in her own way. So she'd given up the dream of Jonah.

If she hadn't, she wouldn't have Nathan.

Elise shook off the melancholy thoughts and settled down under the blanket. If she stayed there too long she was going to end up falling asleep.

* * *

Jonah rubbed at his damp hair and tossed the towel on the rail, not bothering to straighten it. He strode through the house and found Parker in the kitchen. "How long does Fix think this is going to take?"

His face hurt now, and he'd had to take an awkward shower, washing the cuts but not reopening them.

Parker said, "He's waiting on a call."

Jonah crossed to the coffeepot, knowing it was decaf, since Parker never had caffeine. Jonah even stocked it just on the off chance his teammate was at his house. He filled a cup. "Whoever killed the reporter couldn't hit Elise at the mailbox. He tried again with the car, twice, and those attempts didn't work. He'll be gunning for us now."

Parker said, "If it's not tonight, I'll have Fix put in a call. There's a chance the trader will realize something is up, but Fix will just have to finesse it."

"Thanks."

"Your girl's on the couch." Parker walked to the door. "I'll be on the perimeter for the next half hour."

Jonah watched him go and then went to the living room. Elise was curled up on her side, one hand under her cheek. He lifted her as gently as he could. "Time for bed."

It was past time for her to be in the guest room. Especially with cracked ribs.

"Thanks, Martin."

Jonah shut his eyes as the words hit him like a blow.

THIRTEEN

Elise watched from the window as Hailey Shelder's car pulled up out front. She wasn't going to fly out the door and hug her son to death, even though she wanted to. With teenagers you had to play it cool and wait for them to let you know what they needed. Then you could ignore it and do what you wanted, after you'd respected their "needs."

Shelder opened the door but kept her eyes on Jonah's land while Nathan stepped inside. He dropped his backpack by the door.

Elise got in his space and wrapped him up in her arms. When had he gotten so tall?

"Uh-oh." Nathan chuckled. He leaned back and put on a ridiculous high voice. "It's been less than twenty-four hours, but you don't care. I'm so big. You've missed me so much."

Elise shoved his shoulder playfully. "Smarty-pants."

It was laugh or cry. She hadn't even seen

Jonah yet that morning. He'd been in his home office—which technically should be the dining room—all morning, talking on the phone and basically ignoring her.

Elise turned back to Hailey. "Thank you so much."

Nathan trailed straight for the kitchen, being a big fan of second breakfast. Hailey said, "He's a good kid. Kerry seems to think so, too. My thirteen-year-old has developed a terminal crush on your son." Hailey laughed. "Nathan seemed to take it pretty well."

Elise smiled. "I bet that was interesting."

"She actually stopped playing with her puppy for five whole minutes, just to stare at him."

Elise chuckled.

"Shelder. In my office." Jonah's voice was a boom down the hall.

Hailey glanced at Elise, a frown on her face.

Elise whispered, "I have no idea. He won't even speak to me."

Hailey went to Jonah's office, and he shut the door.

Elise sighed, figuring that was pretty much how their whole relationship had been—one giant closed door. *Is that what I'm supposed to think, God? Maybe he doesn't feel the way I feel, and he never has. Jonah was everything I wanted for so long. Now that I have him back in my life, I don't know if I can let him go again.*

Maybe she just needed to be content with them being friends only. She didn't think her heart could handle that, not considering the fact they were going to be in each other's lives now. Forever linked by Nathan. The only question was exactly how hard it would be to continue to see him and never be able to tell him how she'd always felt.

Because despite the four years she'd been married to Martin, Elise had always been in love with Jonah. As horrible as it made her, and as bad a decision as that was, Martin had been good to her. Elise never deserved even his meager attempts at being a husband. He'd tried at least. He'd loved her, and she'd never reciprocated it the way he'd wanted.

She didn't know what would've happened to them, had he lived. Perhaps she'd have grown to love him better, for their son's sake. Or maybe she would have told him her true feelings—that her need for acceptance was so powerful, she'd been swept away by the first person who'd offered to always be there for her.

Whatever the outcome of her telling him the truth, it would have upended all of their lives. She probably would have lost Nathan to Martin and his family.

"Mom, you okay?"

She nodded but didn't look at him. He would know she wasn't fine.

Elise wandered to where she'd left her Bible on the coffee table and flicked again to the verse she'd read that morning in *Romans*.

But God shows His love for us in that while we were still sinners, Christ died for us.

Elise shut her eyes. *Thank You.* She wasn't perfect, not by any stretch of the imagination, but she was loved by God. She'd found her worth not in chasing after the ease of riches the Rivers family had seemed to have, or in being loved and accepted by people—even though she did have that from Nathan. She'd found God's love was powerful enough to fill all the empty, lonely places inside her.

She'd grieved her husband, loved her son and tried to forget about Jonah. To forget about the wrong she'd done. Finding God was a blessing she couldn't even dream of ever deserving, and that was the beauty of it.

"Time to go."

Elise jerked from her thoughts and turned. Hailey strode behind Jonah with a look on her face that made Elise bite her lip to keep from laughing. Apparently Hailey didn't know what on earth was up with Jonah, either.

Elise pulled her boots on while Jonah and

Hailey stepped outside. Nathan strode from the kitchen, his mouth full and a half-eaten burrito in his hand.

"Jonah said it's time to go."

"'Kay."

Elise heard something in his voice, but she had to wait for the right time if she was going to draw him out. When she gripped the door handle, Nathan stopped her.

"Mom?"

She glanced at him, saw the crinkles of concern on his face. "Yes, honey?"

He shook his head and the look dissipated. "Never mind."

Nathan went out first, and Elise followed. Jonah and Hailey were between the house and a nondescript black SUV with government plates. Because that wouldn't stand out in ranch country. Still, Elise pulled back her reaction to their imposing vehicle when she saw how intent Jonah and Hailey were on the area around them.

Despite how he seemed to feel about her this morning, Jonah was still protecting her.

The warm feeling fought with the hurt of being ignored as she walked to the car and they drove to the zoo.

Elise wasn't going to get caught unawares again. At every corner they turned, she looked back. Hailey did the same. Even Nathan was nervous, but he purged that feeling not by being hyperalert, but by texting faster.

He glanced up, smiling. "Theresa might come and visit at Thanksgiving."

"That's great, honey."

"That your girlfriend?" Jonah's tone made Elise shift in her seat.

Nathan shook his head. "Not really. Just a friend."

Great. Was he going to ask why Nathan hadn't gotten this girl to be his girlfriend? Like her son didn't have plenty of interest from girls. He was simply handicapped by the fact that Elise had dragged him one state west, and soon enough he'd be leaving for college. Hardly conducive to a serious relationship, even if she did think that was appropriate for a teenager— which she was on the fence about in the first place. But it happened. She'd been married in her late teens.

If Jonah didn't know teenagers were complicated, and their relationships infinitely more so, he was going to have to catch up fast. Elise could barely keep up, and she spent every day with her son.

Hailey was smirking.

"What?"

"Mama bear just showed her face."

Elise scowled, knowing she was also smiling. It was a different kind of mad altogether, and Hailey knew exactly how Elise felt, since her daughter had been in danger, too. That was how Hailey and Eric got together, during a different manhunt, and she'd told Elise the whole story.

All she could do now was thank God Nathan hadn't been targeted in any of this. If he had, she'd have figured out a way to get him away from town. It would have meant him leaving on his own, in secret, but she would have dealt with the worry, knowing he was safe.

So far she'd been the only one—aside from the reporter—who was targeted. Jonah's presence in the car both times included him, sure, but that was more like collateral damage. She was the one the trader wanted to get rid of.

Just because she'd been in the office? Because she'd been hired back?

Or for another entirely different reason?

Jonah parked the car outside the zoo, as close as he could get to the gate. Elise's whispered voice speaking his brother's name would not get out of his head. He wanted to hit his forehead on the steering wheel, or turn the radio up as loud as it would go, just to try and jog it loose.

He was jealous of a dead man.

That was what it all boiled down to, and it irked him in a way he could not believe. Had he ever been this mad before in his entire life?

The kicker was, Jonah wasn't mad at Elise at all. She'd grieved his brother, was probably still grieving in a way. He didn't blame her for her memories. How could he? It was himself he was mad at. Jonah couldn't fault her for the choices she'd made, even if he didn't understand them one bit. He had a nephew because of her relationship with Martin.

He wouldn't be jealous of a dead man.

With a low growl, Jonah climbed out. He held the door open while Elise did the same, blinking against the early-morning light. Because the bulletproof windows in the SUV he'd ordered were tinted. It had cost him several favors and a lot of begging, but he'd wrangled a safer vehicle for the duration of this operation.

Elise was going to be protected.

But right now she would be safe with Hailey. He turned to his teammate. "You stick with Elise. Nathan can go with me." Then he turned to her. "The foreman is due this morning, right?"

Elise nodded. "That's what Dom told me."

"Okay. Nathan, I'd like to check the perimeter and all the exits. That sound okay?"

"Sure." The teenager flicked the fall of hair

on his forehead from his eyes and shot his mom
a look. Jonah didn't know what it meant until
he saw Elise smile.

Was it too much effort for them to use words?
Even Hailey and Elise did it. Communicating
perfectly well with a look, or the bare minimum
of words. It infuriated him to be left out of the
rapport they'd established. He didn't think he'd
ever understand what went on between them
all, which with Nathan and Elise was reason-
able. They'd had each other for years, so how
had Elise managed it with Hailey so soon?

Nathan trailed after him. Jonah watched the
area to see if anything had been moved, or dis-
turbed at all. The gates were still open, and it
didn't look like anyone had been at the zoo
since they'd found Fix here the day before.

Nathan's phone chirped. He pulled it out
and tapped buttons before sliding it in his back
pocket.

"Same girl?"

"Same girl." Nathan kept walking beside
him. "Theresa Walker. We went to youth group
together, at my church, so I've known her pretty
much forever."

"You like her?"

Nathan shrugged. "Doesn't matter either
way. If it works, if we can figure out how to
be in the same state, then fine. But she's in

Idaho and I'm, like, eight hours away. It's not like we can go see a movie. I'll be in college. She's working on her dad's farm and going to school there."

"So you're not planning to get married young like your mom and dad?"

Nathan's gaze turned distant. "Didn't exactly work out for them, did it?"

"I'm sure your mom did the best she could."

"That's not even what I'm talking about. I know exactly how my mom lived, survived and managed to smile through it. I was there."

Jonah wanted to ask the kid what his problem was but didn't think it would be received well. They'd been on good terms with the motorcycle, and after. What had changed? As far as Jonah was concerned, Nathan was a blessing in his life. The last part of Martin he'd never thought he would get the chance to know.

"As far as I see it, either I get married young and risk winding up like my mom, or I don't and I risk winding up like you." Nathan's eyebrow rose. "Wanting something I can't have."

"Let's check out these buildings." Hailey motioned to the feed and treatment centers. "We'll be able to see if the foreman comes from the windows."

Elise nodded and headed for the portable

buildings, and the two-story structure behind that should have been a barn. It had that look about it, and likely housed equipment, and extra construction supplies probably warped and useless from the floodwaters by now. She hadn't even been in there yet.

Anything was better than dwelling more on why Jonah wouldn't even look at her, let alone talk to her about anything more than business.

She walked around the portables, which would probably fall down if she even tried to go inside, and made her way to the barn.

Hailey held her arm out. "I'll go first."

"I'll bring up the rear. You know, because the last person in line never gets picked off first."

Hailey laughed. "Thankfully this isn't a bad horror movie." Still, she got out her gun.

"Agreed." She even shivered.

The empty, ruined buildings were so bad, Elise could barely move around without having to step over something. She was going to need all the funding the mayor had allocated, and maybe more, if she hoped to finish this project. She might as well be starting from scratch and building a brand-new zoo—except for the fact they had to clear away remnants of the old one first.

Hailey whistled.

"That's what I was thinking. It's going to

take another natural disaster to clean all this away." Elise stepped over downed equipment and around feed barrels. Hailey went a different direction, her footsteps fading under the sound of Elise's steps and the clatter of metal rods.

Elise found the stairs at the back. "I'm going to check out the loft!"

"Be careful!"

The stairs were still intact, a good sign. Elise held the rail, praying it wouldn't all collapse out from under her feet. Finally she reached the top, where the air was a good ten degrees cooler. The window had been smashed out, and cages were stacked along one wall. The majority of the room was clear, but for a few piled-up cardboard boxes that had *Christmas lights* and *Decorations* scrawled on the side in permanent marker.

She wandered to the shattered window and looked out. Cold air whipped at the collar of her coat. The lake was right below her, adding to the rustic look of the zoo. Repainting it, she'd be able to do a whole ranch theme, and maybe go heavy on the petting-zoo angle, rather than cater toward more exotic animals that could only be observed from behind thick glass. Kids loved a more hands-on experience, like feeding goats and sheep from their hands.

Jonah and Nathan were across the lake, but she didn't know if they saw her.

A floorboard creaked up the stairs.

"Come and check out the lake," Elise said. She looked back out, watching to see if Nathan was going to spot her. When he did, she waved.

But Nathan's wave was more frantic. Jonah put his hands to his mouth and yelled... What, she didn't know. Was she supposed to be able to hear him? She pulled out her phone and turned to tell Hailey the two of them were acting bizarre.

The knife flashed as it swooped down at her.

Elise was still turning, so it glanced off her shoulder. Fire sliced through her upper arm and the momentum sent her sprawling backward. A masked man in a dark green army jacket grinned. Elise's shoulder clipped the window and she screamed. One arm flailed as she fell.

And then she hit the water.

FOURTEEN

A flash in the window was all Jonah saw before Elise fell. Beside him, Nathan choked, "Mom!" The teenager ran the path around the lake.

Jonah followed, arms and legs pumping. When Nathan dived into the lake, the dirty water filled with who knew what debris, Jonah prayed. And he kept running.

He had to find Shelder and get to the man who'd pushed Elise out the window. As much as it pained him that he couldn't be the one to get Elise from the lake and make sure she was okay, he had to do his job first. Nathan was here and able. But he'd never felt torn like this before.

God, help both of them. The prayer felt awkward, but he pushed the feeling aside.

Jonah pulled his gun. Cautiously and as fast as possible, he entered the barn. Shelder was in the process of standing. He caught her elbow until she had her balance. "Got it?"

She nodded, touching a finger to the side of her head. That was when he saw the blood. "Hit you on the head?" When she nodded, he said, "He ran out the door?"

"Didn't see. Go get him."

Jonah cleared the barn first, in case the man had hidden instead of running. It only took minutes before he was preceding Shelder outside. Hailey was already on her phone, calling in what had happened and asking for an ambulance.

Nathan, dripping wet, led an equally soaked Elise from the water, both of them coughing. Hailey stowed her phone in her jacket and went to meet them while Jonah circled the immediate area, looking for any sign of where the attacker had gone.

He glanced back to where Elise sat on the ground with Nathan beside her. She had her jacket off her shoulder and Nathan was pressing something against the outside of her arm. She was hurt? Hailey crouched beside them, but Jonah had to search for the suspect.

He'd never hated his job more than he did in that moment.

With a brisk pace, he traced every exit from the barn with no sign of the suspect, or a car. He needed to get as much of a description from

Elise and Hailey as they had to put out an alert to local law enforcement. Nothing else could make any good come from this than if they got a usable lead that would give them a shot to catch this guy.

Parker and Hanning pulled into the parking lot. He waited while they strode toward him.

"What happened?"

Jonah motioned back to where Hailey, Elise and Nathan were. "Let's go find out."

They started walking, and Eric said, "Hailey's okay?"

It was the only concession the man gave to the fact that their teammate was his fiancée. And it impressed Jonah. If Elise was on their team, he would never allow her to be put in harm's way. Yet Eric trusted that Hailey could take care of herself—that she was as much a trained marshal as he was.

Jonah said, "Bump on the head."

Unlike Hailey, Elise was not trained. She didn't know how to effectively fight for her life. How could she? She'd never had to defend herself. That was why Jonah had to stand guard.

His dad would even say that God had brought them together now, when she needed him the most. Whether that was true, or not, Jonah didn't know. It was a nice thought, given that he wanted Elise to be safe. And he was the one who was going to take care of her. *I'm okay with it, God. I'm glad You've put me here.*

Now that he was talking to the Lord again, he could admit God might have a plan going. That He'd designed for Jonah to be here with Elise and Nathan when they needed a protector.

Thank You for gifting me with this job.

Because it was a gift. Elise's friendship was a gift, if he could still have it. His relationship— if he could build something good—with his nephew was a gift.

And he would cherish both.

He stopped in front of Elise and took the cloth from Nathan. It was the teenager's balled-up undershirt. Nathan's eyes were wide, his pupils dilated.

"Sit, yeah?"

Nathan nodded, tumbling on to the concrete so Jonah had to steady him with a hand on his shoulder.

Elise's face was pale also, her breaths short and sharp. Behind him, he could hear Eric and Hailey murmuring to each other. He didn't want to hear what they were saying when it would make him wish for something he could never have. Elise would always love Martin.

"Jonah." Pain had drawn lines around her mouth.

He realized he was squeezing her arm in

his grip. He knelt on the concrete. "We have to keep pressure on it. An ambulance will be here soon."

She nodded, her lips pressed into a white line.

Jonah turned only his head, only to see Hailey with her eyes on him. Eric pressed a handkerchief to her forehead and she winced. He asked her, "What happened?"

She gritted her teeth. "He came out of nowhere. Totally silent. I could hear Elise moving around upstairs and I was about to head up there, but there was a door I was trying to clear the way to, for a second exit. I felt him there more than I heard anything. When I turned he slammed something into my head."

Jonah wanted to rail at her for being caught unawares, but he figured Eric would have that talk with her—after he'd made sure she was okay. That was the only thing that stopped him, aside from the fact she looked like she was about to throw up.

Sure enough, Hailey pushed away Eric's hand, turned around and puked.

"Concussion." Parker pulled a bottle of water from his coat pocket and handed it to her, but Eric intercepted it. "Thanks."

Jonah turned to Elise. "Are you hurt anywhere else, or just your arm?"

She had bruised ribs already, and plenty of grazes from their near misses the past couple of days. She'd hardly needed this to add to it.

Elise shook her head, but her eyes filled with tears. "The water—" Her voice cracked.

Nathan said, "It was full of debris. When I got to her, she was tangled in weeds."

Elise sucked in a choppy breath that made him want to pull her into his arms in a hug. Before he could, Nathan wrapped his mom up in a comforting hold while Jonah tried to keep his grip on her injured arm.

The siren signaling the ambulance drew closer.

"Help is here." He could hear how flat his voice was, and he hated it. Elise needed comfort, but it wasn't like he was going to be the one to give it to her.

It was just a matter of inches and the knife would have made it into her heart. Inches and she would've been a dead woman.

Elise whimpered. Jonah couldn't fight it anymore. He placed Nathan's hand on the compress on her wound, and touched her face instead. "I am very, very glad that you're okay."

"Me, too."

If he hadn't seen her fall, they wouldn't have been able to pull her from the water in time. If she hadn't seen them from the window, Elise wouldn't have turned in time to see the attacker and been able to move aside.

Next time, he was going to be there.

Next time, he would make sure he was standing between Elise and her attacker.

Next time, Jonah would take a bullet for her.

But as she turned to Nathan and sought comfort from her son, what he realized she needed was someone to love her.

Too bad she would never let him.

Elise watched while the doctor finished up the stitches in her arm, slathered goo on it and stuck a bandage on top. Parker stood by the door, arms folded across his chest like this was another day at the office.

Nathan held her good hand with one of his and texted with the other. Apparently his mom getting cut was big news. She squeezed his hand, and he did the same in return, glancing her way. She was glad her son had stayed with her. Not that he could have gone anywhere else, but she knew he wanted to be here.

Unlike a certain other person, who had touched her like she was the most precious thing in the world and said sweet words while he looked in her eyes. And then Jonah just switched it off. Got up and went to work. Leaving her with macho Parker for a bodyguard.

What was up with *that*?

Leaving her to be checked out by the EMTs, not even waiting to know if the cut was serious. Or to find out the extent of her bruises. No, he left her to talk with Detective Manners and his smarmy partner, to tell them what had happened.

She'd wanted to send Nathan somewhere out of the way so he didn't hear it, but he'd insisted he was fine. How much more of this was her son going to be able to tolerate before he freaked out at the prospect of losing his mother, leaving him with no parents? He missed his dad, even though it was also hard because he'd never actually met Martin. She'd told him everything she remembered, many times over, and every year they'd had cake on Martin's birthday. But that wasn't the same as having a dad in his life.

If Jonah wanted to fill that position as Nathan's uncle, he was going to have to actually stick around instead of leaving for work at every opportunity. Clearly the fact that he intended to protect her was all talk. He seemed to be leaving it to his team, like she was just another witness on a case who didn't mean anything to him.

"All finished."

She gave the doctor a small smile. "Thanks."

"I'll get you scripts for ibuprofen and an antibiotic to fight off any infection, and you'll be good to go." He leaned toward her for a second, a gleam of humor in the eyes shaded by bushy gray eyebrows. "I expect to not see you back for any other injuries anytime soon. Okay, missy?"

She laughed. "I'll try."

It wasn't like she could control the fact that someone kept attempting to kill her. But she could control what was happening at the zoo, and the danger that lay there.

"Let's go."

Parker's eyebrows rose, as though he didn't intend to move until he decided to do so. "Where to?"

"I want to talk to the mayor."

Her voice was steady, but the residue of fear was like a dark cloud at the edges of her vision. Like being in a tunnel. Jonah's presence had helped, but now that he was gone, she was being sucked in.

Like the water.

She'd thought the knife and the fall were the worst part—until she'd hit the lake.

Freezing cold had sucked the fight from her. Then she'd tried to move, tangled in weeds. She'd kicked out with her legs, only to jar them against something hard, shooting pain up to her hips.

Elise shivered. Parker handed her the change of clothes someone had brought her. That weirded her out, but maybe it had been Jonah who went through her things. Or a female marshal. Another stranger going through her bags and seeing the sorry state of her wardrobe.

Parker drove them downtown. He led the way to the mayor's office like he was a professional bodyguard. Like Elise was actually someone important.

The receptionist, a perky girl who looked barely older than Nathan, looked up. "Can I—"

"No." Elise strode past a chuckling Parker and walked straight into the mayor's office. "Dom?"

His chair dwarfed him, his dark hair shiny in the fluorescent light. "I'll call you back." He ended the call on his cell phone and set it on the desk in front of him. Dom got up and circled the desk, one arm outstretched toward the chairs. "You look like you should sit down."

Elise took one of the seats. Energy bled from her as she realized how much effort she'd been using just to keep herself upright and alert. "I need to talk with you."

Nathan took the other seat while Dom perched on the end of the desk. Parker had taken up residence by the door, hands across his chest again. Was that his go-to pose? Maybe it wasn't just because it showcased his muscles. Or maybe he was that shallow. She would probably never know the answer.

"Uh… Mom?"

Elise blinked. Parker smirked, which made her roll her eyes at him out of embarrassment. Was he going to tell Jonah she'd been staring?

She turned to Dom. "We won't be returning to the zoo." Not just because she'd nearly died. "There are too many hazards for anyone to be walking around. I need the construction crew to clear everything out first. Then we will be able to go in."

"Ah, yes." Dom scratched his impressively trimmed facial hair. "About that. Well, the foreman called me a short while ago. I was about to come looking for you. Are you okay?"

He didn't need the ins and outs of what had happened to her. "What did the foreman say?"

"It's about the lion."

Nathan said, "You mean the tiger, Shera?"

Dom nodded. "The crew won't go in the zoo unless the animal has been caught. I know it's loose, and so far hasn't hurt anyone. Thank the good Lord. But the crew refuses to come in unless you catch the tiger first." He glanced at Parker, then back at her, his voice suddenly low. "People are starting to notice. They know she's not dangerous, but a tiger can't be free to roam."

"Shera is very dangerous."

Dom blinked. "I was under the impression she was old, and blind."

"That doesn't mean a four hundred-pound animal isn't dangerous. She takes a swing at anyone and they lose. I'm genuinely worried she'll come across a kid wandering the woods." Elise didn't have time to be hurt, or tired. "I'll take care of that first thing tomorrow."

"Mom—"

"We'll take care of it."

Nathan shook his head. "That wasn't what I was objecting to."

She knew he was worried if she could do it without two weeks of bed rest. But what other choice was there? Animal control could help, but they'd let it go this long. They simply weren't prepared for a loose animal of Shera's nature.

"I want the crew in there ASAP."

Dom scratched his jaw again. What was wrong now? "I understand the need, but you don't look capable of doing this without help."

Elise shifted, ready to fire back even if it was the truth. But he cut her off.

"Nevertheless, I understand the urgency. We

need this tiger deal wrapped up so you can get to work."

"Thank you."

"I'll ask Bernadette if she knows of anyone who might be able to help you."

Elise stilled. "I don't need her help."

"Still, I'll ask her, anyway. She might be of assistance in this case. She does know most of the people in town, and she's worked on fund-raisers for the zoo before."

"That's interesting." Elise knew she should close her mouth, but pain plus the meds the doctor had given her meant she had no filter. "I'm glad she found something to do with the money she stole from me."

Dom leaned back for his phone and pressed a bunch of buttons. Then he looked up at her. "My wife has done serious wrong to you in the past, but that is the reason she is going to be involved in this."

"She doesn't have anything to do with me being back here, or my working for this town."

Dom's eyes widened knowingly. "She doesn't?"

"You hired me."

He didn't say anything. Elise was beyond caring what Bernadette intended to do. She wasn't interested in her mother-in-law trying to "fix" things between them. "Did she hire me back with my husband's money?"

Nathan reacted, but Elise couldn't stop it now.

"With his death benefit? His life-insurance money that I should have been able to use to feed and clothe Martin's son? Money that your wife—Nathan's own grandmother, the richest person I know—*stole* from me?"

Dom sputtered.

The door flung open. Jonah stalked across the room. "You didn't need to text me, Dom. Parker already did." He turned his dark look toward her. "You're done."

"What?"

He hauled her up. Thankfully, using her good arm. His grip wasn't painful, but she wasn't getting out of it without a fight. As he dragged her by Nathan, Elise saw tears on her son's face. He swiped them away, and she saw the look of disapproval on Parker's face.

"I'll stay with Nathan," he said.

She turned back, still being pulled along by Jonah. Nathan wasn't coming with her?

FIFTEEN

Jonah slammed the door to the SUV and strode around to Elise's side. He flung the door open and waited for her to get out. He restrained himself, he didn't even tap his foot.

Elise and his mom were going to get things straight once and for all.

It was part of protecting her—that was how he saw it. She was hurting enough, she didn't need the stress of his mom's lies on top of it. He was as mad as she was that his mom hadn't given her money she was supposed to have had, but the look on Nathan's face was what had put him over the edge.

After Parker had sent him that text, he'd rushed over from Fix's house. The first thing he'd seen was Nathan, and the hurt in the teenager's eyes was more than Jonah could take. So he did the thing he always did—he fixed the problem.

Jonah took Elise's elbow, wondering if this

was, in fact, a good idea. He stopped and turned to her, pointing at his mother's front door. "If we go in there, you're seeing this through to the end. You can't chicken out in the middle of it. So if you're not up to this, or if you want to regroup and do it later, then tell me now and we'll walk away."

Elise lifted her chin. "I want to know what she has to say for herself."

The front door opened, and his mom stood there. Her dress was cut well to accentuate her slim figure, and around her neck was a string of pearls Dom had given her on their first anniversary. He supposed some might find her intimidating, with her expensive clothes and power haircut. Jonah saw her as "Mom."

Sure, she'd always had the housekeeper clean up when he was sick as a kid. And the chef was the one to make him chicken soup. That wasn't the point. She was the one who sat with him on his bed and watched cartoons with him when he didn't feel well.

If Jonah and Martin were both sick, she'd let them sleep in her bed. His dad had joked about being kicked out to the guest room, but he'd understood. It wasn't until Elise came into their lives that Jonah started to see a different side of his mother—a side he didn't like.

His mom's eyes were on the woman at his side. "Hello, Elise."

No turning back now, he supposed. Elise was going to have to finish what she'd started in the office. She'd have to get all her facts—and her emotions—straight before they made sure Nathan was okay. Parker would keep him physically safe, but emotionally, who knew how he was doing?

"Can we talk to you, Mom?"

She smiled, a softness that he didn't think he'd ever seen before. "Sure, honey." His mom held the door wide, and then escorted them to one of the front sitting rooms. "Please have a seat." Her gaze settled on Elise. "Are you okay, dear?"

Elise did not look well. Jonah sat beside her on a dainty couch that made him feel like he'd just walked through a muddy field. He took her hand because he wanted to. They were here so she could move past this and finally get some rest while he ran down the person trying to kill her.

Jonah pulled out his phone. No missed calls—as if he wouldn't hear his ringtone. But his frustration had been loud in his ears. He didn't even know if Elise had tried to say anything to him during the car ride to his mom's house—he'd been that determined to get this over with.

Across from them, his mom wrung her hands together. "Do you want me to tell you why you're back in town?"

Elise took a breath, like it was strength. "Yes, I would, Mrs. Rivers." Elise had always been polite to his mom, even when Bernadette was tearing her down in front of her society friends.

His mom nodded, not even correcting Elise on the fact that she'd taken her husband's name. "When Dom first mentioned the state of the zoo and its need for repair…well, I immediately thought of you. And Nathan."

Jonah's eyes widened. Beside him, Elise sucked in a breath. "You knew about Nathan?"

Bernadette smiled, but where it should have been calculating it was only amused. "Did you really think I would let you go off on your own and not keep track of you?"

"But you kept Martin's death benefits and his life insurance—"

"And his trust fund." Bernadette's smile disappeared. "Let's not forget about that small fortune."

"You kept money I could have used to raise Nathan." Elise shook her head. "Not that I wanted to live large, or for Nathan to be spoiled. I'm glad he knows how to work hard for what he wants, and the value of things you can't buy with money. But I could have used it."

"You did. Or rather, I did."

Elise frowned, her shoulders sinking as though she didn't have the energy to hold herself up. Jonah shifted so she was leaning against him. She said, "What do you mean?"

"I had a man keep track of you. He reported to me you were pregnant, so when you had Nathan, I paid off the hospital bill. Small things like that. But after several years I realized the extent of the wrong I'd done you. I knew I couldn't approach you, you'd never have accepted the money when you felt like you were handling your life. And you would have kept Nathan from me if you could."

His mom sighed. "The PI told me when you needed anything. Like when Nathan broke his leg, and the time the sanctuary couldn't afford to pay you and your electricity bill was due, and suddenly paid off. All that was me. Trying to help."

Having a financial guardian wasn't something that went unnoticed. Elise had simply figured it was the help of her local church.

She lifted her chin. "Trying to pay off your guilt?"

His mom's smile was small. "You could say that."

"Is that why you had Dom hire me? So you could pay for Nathan's college tuition?"

"Your job pays your salary. But the Martin Rivers Memorial Scholarship is a different story. His trust fund has helped more than forty young men and women go through college who otherwise would never have been able to afford it." She sighed. "I'm sorry. I'm trying to make amends, to be a better person. This is my overbearing way of fixing what I've done."

His mom was quiet for a moment, and then she said, "I'm asking for your forgiveness, Elise. No amount of money can buy it, I know that."

"The old you would have done exactly that. Thrown money at the problem until you felt better about yourself."

Jonah saw the joy brighten his mom's eyes. "You could say I've seen the light."

Elise stiffened. "You helped in your way, and I'm grateful for that. But the reality is you've always resented my presence in your life. Why would now be any different when I'm still the same me I always was? Nathan can't fix what's wrong with you."

"I'm not asking him to." Bernadette shook her head gently. "But I would love the opportunity to get to know my grandson."

Jonah smiled. "He's a great kid. And we should get back to him. He was pretty upset when we left."

Elise stood, glancing between them. "If he's upset, it's because he's been put through the wringer by the two of you."

She took a step back, her attention zeroing in on his mom. "Thank you for your apology. It's been a harrowing few days, and I need to get back to my family."

Elise walked out, leaving Jonah with a sick feeling in his stomach.

He opened his mouth to tell his mom bye when his phone rang. The display said Ames. Jonah clicked to answer the call. "Rivers."

"Fix set the meet."

Elise set the plates on the table. "I'd rather not talk about your mother right now."

Wasn't it obvious she was still processing that whole conversation? Or she was apparently supposed to swallow the mouthful of secrets Bernadette had kept, and simply move on. Either way, Jonah needed to catch on to the fact she couldn't do that. She just wasn't wired to roll with the punches. Elise had to reason things out.

Jonah pulled the store-bought lasagna from the oven and set it on the table. It smelled really good. If this was the extent of Jonah's bachelor cooking abilities, it was fine with her. They'd be actually equal on something instead of her feeling, at every turn, like he had the upper hand.

He looked disappointed she didn't want to talk, but she couldn't take that on board along with everything else, so she focused on cutting the food and dishing it out. Nathan was at Parker's house for the night, wherever that was. He'd texted to tell her the marshal had a *sick* gaming system, and he'd be *fine*. Like that was supposed to reassure her.

Jonah sat, and she prayed silently before she began eating. When she looked up, his eyes were fixed on her. "What?"

"You could have said grace, I wouldn't have minded."

"Oh, okay." Since he was willing, and she needed it, Elise reached over and held his hand. His strong, warm hand. *Don't think about that.*

She said grace, asking for continued protection, and for God to reveal Himself to them. It was good to see what He was doing. When she wasn't sure what else to say, Elise closed the prayer. There were things going on in her head Jonah just didn't need to know.

He took a bite of food, his attention never leaving her. When he'd swallowed, he said, "Is there anything you want to ask, about the meet with Fix?"

Elise didn't think he wanted to hear what she

thought. Hailey had called her "mama bear" earlier, and the moniker wasn't exactly inaccurate. Jonah didn't need to know she'd taken that on board for him, too. He'd think she distrusted the fact he could be safe. He was a trained marshal. He could, and would, take care of himself.

Why did she care? It wasn't like she was in love with him.

"I can see the wheels turning." Jonah set his fork down and held her hand, much the same way she'd held his during the prayer. "This is the best way to find out who the trader is, and put a stop to these continued attempts on your life."

"I know that."

"Do you want to keep almost getting killed?"

"Of course not. How can you ask me that?"

"You need to let me do this, Elise."

She bit her lip, and to her dismay, tears filled her eyes. Jonah pushed his chair back and crouched beside her. "Talk to me."

She set her elbows on the table and put her head in her hands. Taking a deep breath was all she had the strength to do. Jonah's hand rubbed up and down her back. "You can trust God that I'll come through this, right?"

Because he didn't think she could trust him? Or because he didn't think God would make her

suffer the death of someone she cared about…
again.

Elise turned to him. "Do not get hurt."

To his credit, he didn't smile. "I wasn't planning on it."

"I know you aren't, but—"

"Look." He squeezed her shoulder. "Fix is meeting the trader and I'm going along for the ride. Fix will accept a shipment tomorrow night and I'll be there under the guise of helping. We'll catch them in the act, and as soon as I give the signal, my team will swoop in and arrest him. The end."

Okay, so he knew how to make it sound simple. "I still don't like you doing this. He killed the reporter. It could be a trap, you know."

Jonah sat back in his seat. "Wow, Ms. Tanner. With all that concern, I might actually think you care about me."

She didn't know whether to laugh or cry. "I've always cared about you, Jonah. That was never the problem."

His eyes darkened. "If that's true, why did you never speak to me after I left?"

Did he really expect an answer that would satisfy him? "Maybe it was *because* you left."

"Well, now I'm back, and so are you."

As if that had fixed anything. "Lo and behold, everything's the same. Your mom still thinks I'm the poor girl from the trailer park. The only reason she wants to make amends is because of Nathan."

"She got saved."

"And now I have to forgive her, or I'm the small one." Elise pushed her plate away. "Why do I always have to be the one to bend for everyone else? My mom. Fix. Your mom. Martin. *You.* The only person in the world who doesn't ask me for anything is Nathan. And he's the only one who has a right to everything I am."

"I'm sorry, Elise." To his credit, he seemed genuine.

"Me, too." She got up, moving to the door. "I'll always be the poor girl you shouldn't be with, and you'll always be out of my league."

"Elise—" He stood. "I need to tell you the real reason I left."

The little dinner she'd eaten churned in her stomach. She needed sleep, but all she would probably get for the effort was restlessness, lingering pain. Nightmares. She sighed. "Let's go sit in the living room."

He nodded, relief washing over his features.

When he was settled beside her on the couch, Elise turned slightly toward him, bracing herself.

Jonah swallowed, his eyes on his hands clasped between his knees. "I knew I had to get space. To figure out who I was. All the usual 'I'm twenty and I haven't found myself yet' stuff. But there was more to it than that. I needed space from you."

She felt her eyes widen. "Me?"

"I couldn't help how I felt about you. I knew you were special from the moment I met you, but there was nothing I could do about it. I was four years older and my dad warned me, over and over, not to do something that would get me in trouble." He blew out a breath between his lips. "The marines seemed like a great way to experience life." He looked at her. "And to give you the time you needed to grow up."

How he felt about her?

As in, the same way she'd always felt about him? And he'd *left*? Elise squeezed her eyes shut. *God, I didn't know that. I could have had everything I ever wanted, but I thought he walked away from me.*

Elise had been right. Jonah would always and forever be out of her league. She straightened, realizing this was her one chance to say what she had to say before he found out what she'd done. "Thank you for protecting me."

He'd protected himself, and he'd obeyed his father. But it was love for her that meant Jonah made the hard decision at an age when that was rare. As painful as it had been to go through,

Elise knew now that he'd made the right decision. For both of them. They hadn't been ready
for a relationship. She hadn't been. And yet it
wasn't long after that she let Martin persuade
her into exactly that.

Jonah squeezed her hand gently, then let go.
"Elise?"

She looked over at him. Was that love for
her in his eyes?

"Will you tell me why you married Martin?"

SIXTEEN

She was up and off the couch before he realized. "I should get to bed. I have to get up and catch a tiger in the morning."

Jonah knew she wasn't feeling good. It was barely nine and she likely did need sleep, but he felt like if they didn't talk about this now, the chance would slip from his fingers. "Don't go, Elise. Don't leave now. I feel we're finally getting somewhere."

She looked…scared. Why, he didn't know. There was obviously something here that she didn't want to get out. "What do you want from me?"

She didn't want to know the answer to that. Jonah wasn't going to put that on her now, when she was hurt and exhausted. He was trying to give her some semblance of peace, since talking to his mother hadn't managed to do so.

Jonah stepped closer to her, just in case her

fear got the better of her and she decided to run. Again.

When he had her attention, he said, "There's a reason why I've never married, Elise. There's a reason why I've never found anyone else." He let that sink in. "When I left for the marines, I knew the next time I saw you that things would be completely different for us. What I didn't know was that it would take this long for that to happen."

Elise was shaking her head even before he was done. "No, I don't believe you. I'm not the reason you've been alone all this time. I can't be. Don't put that on me, Jonah."

"I'm not trying to load you with guilt, and I don't feel like I've been alone. That's not what I'm saying. My life has been full, with work and…" Okay, so there wasn't much else. But part of him felt like maybe he'd always been waiting for Elise. "I'm just really glad you're here now, and I don't want to lose you."

Her face softened. "I don't want to lose you, either."

"Then I need an answer to my question. Now." He waited a second. "Did you love Martin?"

"Yes."

Jonah flinched. He didn't want to betray his true feelings, but it was too late now. He'd already told her the truth of why he left for the marines. If she didn't feel the same way, he would deal with it. Eventually he'd figure out how to get over her, even though in nearly twenty years he hadn't managed it.

"But not in the way you think." She bit her lip and looked down. "Martin…" She sighed. "He understood I didn't love him the way I should have. The way a wife should. He was rebelling. You'd left, and your mother was pressuring him to quit drinking, to quit partying. I think he figured that if he married me it would be the perfect comeuppance to her."

"Why would you say yes to that?" Martin had used her?

She blew out a breath and looked at the window, where the blinds were closed against the night sky. "I didn't think of it like that. All I could think was that I'd get what I'd always wanted. Maybe not exactly what I imagined, but a facsimile of love, and family, at least. I would finally have everything I'd never had growing up."

She looked up at him, her chin raised, daring him to think badly of her. "I was selfish. Looks like I really was just out for the Rivers money, after all."

"Elise—"

"Turns out your mom was right. My mom.

Fix. The whole town. Even Martin knew the real reason we got married. He got to throw it in your mom's face when I moved in to the pool house with him, and I got to pretend I was the princess living large."

"I don't believe you."

"Well, it's true. You're the only one who didn't see it."

"Tell me the truth."

"I just did." She screamed it, and Jonah flinched.

He shook his head. "You were a kid barely out of high school."

"I was an adult."

"That doesn't mean you were mature enough to make that decision. It's why I left. I knew you were too young, and so was I. We both had a lot of growing up to do, and I naively thought you would know. That you'd wait."

"How was I supposed to know that's what you wanted me to do?"

Now, finally, they were getting somewhere. "That stung, didn't it?"

"You know it did."

Jonah folded his arms across his chest, heavy with ache. "I didn't know you'd marry Martin."

"I didn't know you would just leave me, and never look back!" Her face was red, her eyes filled with tears.

"So you just gave up, took the first offer that came along?"

"I had to." She sucked in a breath. "It hurt too much."

"Because I left you?" The ache in Jonah's chest got worse.

"Because you abandoned me to them. Suddenly I had no defense, no one on my side."

"Except Martin."

"He didn't feel the way you did, you know that." She bit her trembling lip. "I was so scared. So alone."

Jonah wanted to gather her in his arms, but he didn't. They had to finish this.

"I knew you'd forget about me and never come back. I knew you'd realize I wasn't worth it, so I married Martin. We were friends at least. But then he *died*. And the kicker is, it was better."

"Being a single mom?"

"I had to rely on God. I had to be strong even though I was so scared, and I did it, Jonah. I did it, and Nathan thrived. I had to know I didn't need you or I'd have always relied on you, for everything. You'd have been my strength, instead of the Lord. It would have torn me apart to live like that, so wrapped up in you."

She swiped the tears from her face. "It hurt. And it was the hardest thing I've ever had to do, but after Martin died, I knew I couldn't be that selfish kid anymore. I needed the space to find out who I was with no one to lean on. I had to know I could take care of Nathan on my own. That I could give and not always expect things to be handed to me. I know I'm not a good person, but now at least I know God loves me and so I can be better. In Him."

Jonah stepped closer. "I loved you with a childish love a long time ago. Now you're grown. You're strong, you're a fantastic mom and a wonderful woman, and it's been a pleasure getting to know you now, Elise."

She looked like she didn't know if she should be happy, or still upset. "But…"

Jonah smiled, touched both her cheeks and held her head in his hands. She was still so little, she brought out all the protective instincts he had inside him. The feelings he had for her now were so much more than before, in maturity and in strength.

"No buts. I just wanted you to know how much of a pleasure this has been. And I'm so sorry you've been hurt." Multiple times, and he hated seeing her scared and knowing she was in danger. "I'm going to make this better for you, because I want us to have the chance to see what could be between us now." He paused a beat. "And I need to know if that's what you want, too."

Elise smiled, even while Jonah wiped tears from her cheeks with his thumbs. "I'd like the chance to see if this could work now."

Jonah lowered his head, finally free to show her how he felt. She'd had enough words from him, and he'd been more open with her than with anyone in his life. But she was special, and she would forever hold that part of him.

When he was a hairbreadth from her lips, the doorbell rang.

Jonah groaned low in his throat and touched her forehead with his. "I'm sure they'll go away if we're quiet."

He felt her shake with silent laughter.

He pressed a quick kiss to her forehead and went to answer the door.

Elise stood back while Jonah opened the door. Deputy Marshal Shelder strode in, a grocery sack swinging from her hand. "Special delivery." Jonah grabbed the sack and rummaged in it before looking up at Hailey, incredulous. "A mullet wig?"

Elise burst out laughing. Jonah's head whipped around and he glared at her. She swallowed the humor and saw Hailey was also fighting it. Elise cleared her throat. "So when's the meeting?"

Hailey answered. "Tonight." But Elise looked at Jonah.

"Seriously?" She was supposed to go to sleep while he went with Fix to catch the animal trader? "Were you planning on telling me this was happening tonight, or was I meant to just wake up tomorrow to find it all over?"

Jonah said, "I was going to tell you."

"Really?" Her mind was spinning, especially after she'd finally admitted how totally selfish she'd been in assuming her chance with Jonah had been over and marrying his brother just to escape her life. Everyone had something they regretted, but hers was like the elephant in the room she couldn't ever escape. Especially not now she was back with Jonah.

Well, with—as in, they were in the same room. Not *with*.

Now that the fog of anticipating his kiss had passed, all the old fears were resurfacing.

"I'm going to go change."

He strode away down the hall, and Elise stood there feeling like a lemon. Did he think she shouldn't worry? That she wasn't scared for him? He was going into a dangerous situation, just like always. It was the choice he'd made, because he was the kind of man who put his life in danger to protect people. But that didn't mean she had to like it.

And it didn't mean she hadn't stayed up many nights over the years, worrying if he was okay. Praying he would be, even if she never saw him again.

The fact that they could be together now was little more than a dream, and everything she'd ever wanted. She knew she didn't deserve it, but everything she had was by the grace of God. Jonah's love wouldn't be any different.

"You okay?"

Elise shook off her thoughts and looked at Hailey. "Sure."

"I didn't…interrupt anything, did I?"

Like Jonah's hands on her face? His lips touching her forehead.

"I did!" Hailey clapped.

Elise laughed. "Don't get ahead of yourself, okay? Things are far from established, but better than they were." She glanced at the closed door to his bedroom. "We cleared the air some."

Hailey had a knowing smile on her face. "I see that."

And though she'd expected Jonah to dislike her for being such an awful person, he didn't. Sure, she tried to be better now. But that was yet more grace.

Jonah strode back out, and Elise burst out

laughing. He'd smashed a beanie on the mullet wig, and his big frame was dwarfed by an even bigger lumberjack shirt so that he looked like a giant. The jeans were standard Western wear over scuffed brown boots.

He narrowed his eyes at her, a glint of humor there. "Don't even say it."

Elise bit her lips together and shook her head.

"Okay, I'm ready." He scratched under the wig and then stowed his phone and keys in his pocket. "Truck?"

Hailey motioned over her shoulder at the front door. "My dad's." She tossed him a set of keys and he caught them in one move.

Elise's stomach lurched, jumping to sit as a lump in her throat. She didn't want to say goodbye, suddenly overwhelmed with wondering if he would come home or not.

Like his brother.

Her goodbye the last time she saw Martin hadn't been the stuff of fairy tales. Most military spouses probably shared an emotional goodbye. Theirs was stilted at best. Martin had been desperate to prove he was as much a man as his older brother. It had taken Elise a long time to swallow the fact that Martin had known she was in love with Jonah.

Especially considering his final words to her. *It isn't like you want me around, Lise.* He'd been at the front door of the pool house, looking back at her over his shoulder. *Maybe while I'm gone you'll discover you feel something for me, too.*

That was when she'd realized Martin loved her the same way she loved Jonah. She'd successfully torn their family apart, and she was going to have to tell Jonah that, too. Eventually he would know the whole truth, and then she would have to put the strength of his feelings to the test. If she didn't walk away again. But what was the point in staying if he didn't love her enough to forgive her of that much?

She would understand completely if he couldn't.

Jonah stopped in front of her. "Get some rest. I'll see you in the morning."

His eyes were serious, but the long hair was almost comical. Elise reached up and straightened the wig and wool hat, so the ends hung to the same length and were not lopsided.

Jonah grinned. "Thanks."

"You're welcome."

The humor didn't last. Standing with Jonah now, saying goodbye, Elise knew she'd been putting off the real reason she had wanted to come home. Now that she was back in town, she needed to visit Martin's grave. She needed to apologize for what she'd done to him, and for her responsibility for his death. To finally say sorry, and a proper goodbye.

Jonah grabbed her hand. He bowed his head and started to pray before she even realized that was what he was doing. His words were rusty, like praying was awkward, but she loved that he wanted to do it. She needed it so badly right now.

When he looked up again, Elise said, "Thank you."

Hailey was still at the door, waiting for Jonah to leave so she could take up her station as Elise's protector for the night. Jonah hesitated, like he wasn't quite ready to go. He wasn't going to kiss her—as much as she might want him to—not while his teammate was in the room.

"I'll see you later?"

Elise nodded. "Be careful."

The door shut, and he was gone. Elise sighed, glanced at Hailey and opened her mouth to say something.

The front door opened. Jonah strode back in, his gaze determined as he walked right up to her. Right into her space.

He pulled her into his arms and kissed her.

SEVENTEEN

Jonah sat in the passenger seat while Fix drove out of town, along the highway that stretched east toward Idaho. He fought for focus, but every so often he remembered the feel of Elise's lips against his, and his mouth curved in a smile.

Fix, on the other hand, was hardly smiling. Elise's brother's hands shook the whole time he gripped the wheel. After an hour, he pulled off onto a dirt road.

Fix had attached a closed trailer to the back of his truck, and Jonah was anxious to get on with the evening's main event. They were going to meet one of the trader's associates, and then transport the animals to the possession of the trader so he could take them out of town.

It should be a simple handoff, but Jonah had to stay alert. So much could go awry.

For now they were in Fix's truck that smelled like take-out fries. Jonah pulled out his phone

and turned the brightness all the way down.
It was how his team was keeping track of his
GPS location, but he didn't need it ringing, so
he turned it to vibrate.

A voice came through the earpiece hidden by
his hair—which made the itchy mullet slightly
more bearable, he had to admit. "Can I get a
microphone check?"

Jonah said to Fix, "You ever meet this guy
before, the trader's associate?"

Fix shook his head.

Through the earpiece, Jonah heard, "I read
you loud and clear."

Elise's brother pulled to the side of the road.
"Never seen the guy, but I've spoken to him
on the phone. Don't know who he is, but he
ain't young."

"This where we meet him?"

Fix nodded.

The earpiece voice said, "Perimeter has been
established, we are now going radio silent."

Jonah had no clue where, in the middle of nowhere on a tiny dirt lane surrounded by trees,
an entire team of marshals was hiding. A he-
licopter was way too noisy, and obvious. Any
vehicle on this road would stick out, and poten-
tially scare away the trader's associate whom
they were meeting. Likely the response time

would be closer to a minute than seconds. He'd have to be on his guard, but that was what operations like this one entailed. The danger was clear, and the chance he could be outed as a federal agent was high.

Headlights in the side mirrors.

Fix cracked his door, so Jonah did the same. The hair and hat covered a lot of his face, but his features still showed. Hopefully whoever this was, he wasn't prevalent in the community, because he'd know exactly who Jonah was.

He kept his head down as the truck—considerably newer than Fix's—pulled up alongside theirs, so the trailers were side by side. A heavy door slammed, and the man strode around the back of the trailer. The face under the ball cap was shadowed, but Jonah saw stubbled cheeks belonging to a man probably in his seventies. Lean, but not taller than Jonah. Green army jacket, just as Elise had described of the flash of her attacker before she'd fallen out the window.

Was this the man who'd shot at her by his mailbox, the man who tried to stab her?

Jonah's hands curled into fists. He stayed beside the trailer and pulled out his phone, out of sight, typing a message with the license plate of the truck and a note about it possibly being Elise's attacker.

The man cracked his trailer door open. "You boys ready to haul all this? There's a beast in here, so you'll be glad there's two of you." His words were chatty, but his tone was anything but.

The voice was graveled, but it did sound somewhat familiar. Still, in the dark it wasn't hard for either of them to hide who they really were.

Jonah kept Fix between him and the trader's associate while they hauled three cages of tiny monkeys, two birds huddled together and a thing that looked like a small brown leopard, but without the spots.

"That one bites."

Jonah glanced over and saw the man was grinning.

"Just kidding."

They stowed the cages in Fix's trailer, which smelled like animal waste. Except when they'd asked prior to tonight, he claimed he'd never done this before. What else had Fix lied about?

"One more."

Jonah strode back to the other trailer and looked inside. At the very back was a huge cage with a sleeping… Shera? The tiger Elise was supposed to catch tomorrow morning was seemingly asleep right in front of him.

"That one'll kill ya soon as look at ya."

Maybe. Four hundred pounds wasn't anything to sneeze at—Elise had explained—but it was old and blind. Did it even have teeth?

He climbed in and tried not to look scared as he moved toward the tiger.

Behind him, Fix laughed. "I'll let you do the honors, dude."

"Thanks." Jonah rolled his eyes. He hauled on the cage, sliding it. The scraping sound was loud in the close confines of the trailer. He stopped, but the animal didn't move. In the beam of the trader's flashlight he saw Shera's nose twitch, and then the visible breath as she blew out hot air into the cold night.

Please, God, do not let her wake up.

They were going to have to lift the cage if they wanted to get it from one trailer to the other. Could the two of them even manage it?

He lifted his end while Fix did the same. When they'd set the cage inside Fix's trailer, the trader's associate said, "You have the address where you're taking these?"

Fix patted his pocket. "Got it right here."

Elise's brother was supposed to drive the animals to the Idaho border, where they'd meet up with the trader. Evidently the man was getting ready to move his operation east, out of state, since things were getting too heated around here.

Jonah just had to catch him before that happened.

"Great." The trader's associate lifted his chin, and moonlight shone on his face.

It was Jonah's neighbor. The old soldier. He'd wondered if Tucker could have been behind the shooting, but his neighbor had claimed an alibi—one the police were supposed to have checked out.

Before Jonah could react, Tucker pulled a Glock with a silencer from behind his back and shot Fix. The muted sound was followed by the thud of Fix hitting the ground.

Jonah crouched to retrieve the revolver from his ankle holster. Tucker swung his leg out in a kick, which Jonah shifted to avoid. He rolled to the side, coming up with his gun out in front of him. They both fired.

The trader flew backward, as did Jonah. He saw stars spread across the sky, and the cloud of his breath puffing out as he tried to breathe against the ache of a bullet hitting his vest. His gun was out of his hand. He shouldn't have let go of it when he fell back, but he couldn't do anything about that now. Was the trader dead?

Jonah looked around for his gun, listening for Tucker's footsteps.

A twig snapped.

Tucker kicked Jonah in the ribs. Jonah didn't see a gun.

He jumped up, ignoring the weight of the bruise pressing on his chest. His fist made contact with Tucker's jaw. The wig shifted, throwing hair across his vision. Tucker kicked out again, a vicious roundhouse. Fire shot through Jonah's ribs, but he stood his ground and threw punch after punch.

Tucker grunted and hit back. The man was strong, even at seventy. There was no way he'd let his military training go. This man was too accurate for that.

But Jonah didn't like losing.

Tucker stumbled back, turning. Jonah readied himself for another punch, but Tucker turned, swinging something in his grip.

The rotten tree limb shattered against Jonah's skull, and he hit the ground.

Hailey's phone rang.

Elise cut off what she'd been about to say and let her answer it. She really liked the female marshal, and they'd been sharing stories of being a single mom. Despite the differences in their kids, and their situations, there were a lot of similarities.

Hailey got up from the couch and put the phone to her ear as she strode toward the hall. "Shelder."

Sam got up off the rug where he'd been snoozing and came to sit beside her. He whined.

"What is—"

The front door blew in.

Elise got up off the couch as Hailey went flying. The marshal hit the ground, and her phone landed three feet beyond her, shattering on Jonah's tile floor. Hailey groaned, her eyes searching the room until they locked on Elise. "Run."

Elise didn't hesitate. Closest to her was the stairs. She didn't think, she just bounded up, followed by Sam.

A boom of noise and the step below her shattered, blasting splinters everywhere. *Sam?* The dog ran past her, as though he'd decided to lead the way instead of following.

Smoke laced the air, and she coughed, her legs screaming with the strain of taking huge steps. She hit the upstairs landing and stumbled, turning right just as the wall at the top of the stairs was hit with another shotgun blast.

Debris showered the hall as she sprinted after Sam—for Jonah's bedroom. She slammed the door shut even though it wasn't much protection against those huge rounds. A phone was beside his bed. She snatched the handset from the base and dialed. There was no tone.

She pressed the buttons, frantic to make it work, but it didn't.

Sam went to the window and barked.

Gunshots from downstairs rang out. They were answered by another blast from the shotgun. Who was chasing her? *God, don't let Hailey get hurt because of me.*

Hailey was still down there. How badly was she injured? Elise didn't hear any more gunshots. Was she dead? Was this guy going to finally kill her, after making Hailey another statistic of a federal agent shot while on duty?

Footsteps bounded toward the bedroom door.

Elise ran for the window, flipped the latch and slid it open. The cold air chilled the sweat of exertion. How could she help Hailey?

The bedroom door flew open and a man with a shotgun stepped in, swinging it one way and then the other. She didn't wait around to see who it was.

Sam jumped out the window. She heard his nails scrabble on the roof overhang above the porch. Elise jumped after him. She hit the porch roof, rolled and slammed against the ground. Pain shot up to her hips and Sam barked.

"Shhh." She forced herself to stand without crying out at the pain and followed him. This guy had tried to kill her so many times over the past few days that there was just no way she'd let him get away with it now. They had to get out of there.

God, keep Hailey safe.

The man bellowed out the window. Elise ran after Sam, the only light coming from Jonah's downstairs windows. Jonah's house wasn't close to anything else, his closest neighbor on the hill. The neighbor's ranch lights were on. Should she head there to call for help? Should she hide in the barn?

Someone grabbed her. "Elise."

It was Parker. Elise forced herself to quit struggling against his grip.

"Let's go."

She went with him, allowing him to drag her along faster than she could run. Around the house they headed toward the back door. Sam glanced back as if to spur them on. "Is Hailey okay?"

"She's doing her job. She'll catch up."

"To us, or the guy with the shotgun?"

She'd have met him on the stairs if she'd come up after him, and he hadn't come out the window. "Is Jonah okay? What's happening?"

Parker yanked on her arm. "You're giving

away our position with your chatter." He scanned the area, then reached up and touched a button on his collar. His voice was low when he said, "Go ahead."

His gaze never stilled, and he repeatedly shifted her so she was behind him. Sam spun in circles, watching every direction for an intruder. Man and dog never stopped moving, and it made Elise's head spin. Her legs were screaming with each movement, but she didn't think she was badly injured beyond bumps and bruises—to go with the passel of injuries she already had.

When was she going to be able to get some rest?

"Copy that."

She looked at Parker. "What now?"

"Jonah was ambushed. The team is on-scene, but he's already gone. The trader's associate took him in Fix's truck with the animals."

So he was alive? "And Fix?"

"Your brother is in critical condition. He's been airlifted to the hospital."

She felt it so strongly, the blow was almost physical. "If Jonah's in danger, why are you here with me? Go and help him!"

Parker's eyebrow rose.

"What are you just standing here for?"

The former SEAL grabbed her arm and hauled her along.

Elise gasped. "Where's Nathan? You were supposed to be keeping him safe. Where is he?"

"Your son is fine. He's at the marshal's office for the night since everyone's on duty." Parker glanced at the night sky, like he was praying for patience.

"We have to go back and help Hailey."

He almost looked as if he agreed, but then he said, "Marshal Shelder can take care of herself, and backup is on its way."

A shotgun blast echoed through the house, followed by a woman crying out.

Elise nearly burst with the need to go help, even though she didn't know how she was supposed to do that.

"Okay." Parker leaned in close. "Run to the barn." He clicked the button on his throat, the one connected to his earpiece. "I'm doubling back for Shelder."

He looked at her. "Go. Now."

Elise didn't wait around. She wanted him to go and help Hailey. Pumping her arms and legs—again—Elise ran for the safety of the barn. The man hadn't come out of the house, right? She'd be safe there.

But what was happening to Jonah?

The catalyst of all this was her. This job.

Her return to town. She'd set all this in motion, hadn't she? It sure felt that way. Jonah wouldn't even be involved if it wasn't for her. He'd have turned the investigation over to the local police and moved on to the next case.

Once again she'd said goodbye to a man and watched him go...to his death.

God, why am I so selfish?

She'd wanted this to be over so badly she'd pushed aside the reality of Jonah being in danger. Sure, he didn't have a "safe" job, but he'd lasted this long because he was good at it. If he got hurt tonight, would he blame her for this, too?

Elise crept into the barn. It was pitch-black, and smelled like a car garage but with an undertone of hay and animals. Hands out in front of her, she felt her way along the outside edge with tentative steps. Still, twice she walked her shin into something. Finally Elise hissed, and stopped.

Sam whined. Apparently he didn't like the dark, either. Did he feel the way she did about spiders? Big animals she could handle, but tiny ones with a million crawly legs? No way.

Parker would make sure Hailey was okay, then he'd come here and get her. It was dark, and she didn't have to hide so much as just crouch behind something. Whoever had the shotgun wasn't going to find her.

The pump action was deafening, echoing in the old barn.

A light flicked on. Brightness filled Elise's gaze, blinding her.

"Gotcha."

EIGHTEEN

The truck jerked to a stop, and Jonah cracked his eyes open to find it was completely dark. Was he in the trailer? Mashed up against a cage, hot air that smelled like raw eggs blasted against his face. He tried to move, and pain shot through his side. He groaned, and the animal replied.

"Nice...whatever you are."

Shera? He hoped not, but at least the thing was in the cage.

Jonah couldn't move away from the animal, tucked as he was in there, tight between two cages with his head by the door. At least as far as he could tell from the way the truck had stopped and the cold air on his neck, presumably from a bad seal in the trailer's door, he'd been thrown in feetfirst. He couldn't decide which he preferred—cold air from outside or warm tiger breath that smelled.

His hands were tied behind his back, his

earpiece had been removed. The wig and beanie were who knew where. His phone—the only way the marshals would know where he was—didn't feel like it was in his back pocket. He tried to reach down with his hands and find out for sure, but didn't have the room to arch his back enough to twist and check both back pockets.

The truck door slammed.

Jonah tensed. Had he ever been in a situation worse than this? Stripped of his weapons, up against someone who could very well best him.

He heard Shera back away and lie still while the trailer door swung open and a shaft of light from outside hit his closed eyelids. Was it morning already?

Hands slipped under Jonah's armpits and hauled him out onto the ground. Jonah slammed against the earth and opened his eyes. They were inside a lit barn, the trailer backed nearly all the way in the door so there was no way anyone outside would be able to see what his neighbor was off-loading.

Where were they? It looked like a normal ranch, but whose?

His neighbor turned, both his hands gripping the barrel of his gun. Was he going to shoot Jonah right here? Jonah didn't especially like the idea of bleeding out onto a dirt floor, all alone. He wanted…

Elise.

And Nathan.

He wanted the chance to live in the way he'd never lived before—a full life with family and laughter. A wife. Kids of his own.

Love.

If it wasn't too late, Jonah was going to do everything in his power to convince her to take a chance on them. But first, he had to get out of here alive.

"Back up."

Jonah twisted so Tucker could see his hands, tied behind him.

Tucker didn't look impressed. He motioned Jonah back with the gun. "Scoot."

Jonah inched back, cataloguing his aches and pains. Fresh bumps and bruises made themselves known, but Jonah kept his face impassive. He'd been shot in the stomach, weeks ago. He had no desire to repeat the experience.

Let Tucker think he was scared. Jonah was merely biding his time, waiting for the man to make a mistake. One that would mean Jonah got the upper hand.

God, help me choose wisely.

The wrong opportunity would mean he'd let

slip his intentions and likely be shot for trying to escape.

Jonah kept moving back, scooting his hips and essentially dragging his legs with him. "If you kill me, the marshals won't ever rest. They'll hunt you forever. Doesn't matter where you hide, they'll dig you out. You can be sure of that."

"Brave words from a man with a gun to his face. Too bad you won't be around to see your buddies play hero." Tucker smirked. He scratched the gray stubble on his chin, pulled off his ball cap and resituated it. "Too bad. Too bad I have a place up north where *no one* will ever find me."

"You think they can't track you in Washington, or are you thinking Alaska?" Jonah kept moving back until his hands found a wooden support beam. He stopped. "Or Canada? Pretty big country, but our extradition is tight. Not like you'd escape justice when you killed a federal agent."

Tucker tipped his head to the side. "Why are you assuming it's only one?"

He'd killed more? Jonah didn't know the man's history, beyond them discussing their military days as neighbors. He'd assumed— from his age—that Tucker was retired. But plenty of older people still worked these days.

Did his nefarious business stretch beyond transporting exotic animals? With his military skills, it could even be possible Tucker was some kind of killer for hire.

"For now, all you need to know is you're going to die. You and your girl will be blamed for this." With a sweep of his arm, he indicated the animals in the trailer. "I'll simply be the frail old man who stumbled across a crime."

He was going to blame them for this? "Not going to play hero and pretend you caught us? Might be some money in a reward if you can return the zoo's animals to the city."

Tucker snorted. "Maybe if these were the zoo's animals. Except Shera, every single creature in that trailer is the real deal. Genuine one hundred percent tradable product. People don't want sickly animals raised in captivity. Especially this dealer. He wants the rush of the wild." Tucker made his opinion known about that, and it wasn't complimentary to his client. "He'll probably get bitten within a week."

Jonah felt around with his fingers, trying to find something sharp to cut the plastic tie. There. A jagged nail in the floor.

"Too bad we're closing up shop, moving it elsewhere, or I'd have been able to stick around and find out what happens to the dealer."

We?

Jonah nodded slowly, like it'd dawned on him. "Didn't figure you for the trader. Guess you're the hired help, standing around waiting for the boss to show and pick up his animals."

"This isn't a trade-off. This is closing up shop." Tucker shifted his grip on the gun. "Tying up loose ends. But I guess you know that, don't you? Fix's big mouth and all. Not that we have to worry about that now."

Jonah's gut churned. Tucker had already killed tonight, and Jonah was next. Then Elise. *God, keep her safe.*

Nathan needed his mom. He'd be upset if Jonah died, but not the way he would grieve if Elise was killed tonight. Especially when Jonah would be left to deal with that failure to protect her. To look his nephew in the eye and know he'd destroyed the teenager's world.

Jonah lifted his chin. "There's no way I'm going to let you walk out of here. You and whoever it is you're working with."

"Big words from a big man, tied up, on the floor, about to get a bullet between the eyes."

Jonah shrugged one shoulder. "What are you waiting for?"

The skin around Tucker's eyes twitched. Jonah had succeeded in surprising him. But he wasn't itching to die. He simply wanted Tucker to make his move, because the jagged edge of the nail was almost through his bindings.

Tucker said, "Guess it's time to die, then."

Jonah swung his leg up and across his body, catching the gun with his boot. He sprang from the floor, hands coming around to grab Tucker's shoulders, bringing his knee up to slam in the shorter man's stomach.

Breath whooshed from Tucker's mouth.

The boom of a gunshot preceded a flash of pain in Jonah's leg. He collapsed with a cry, hot blood flowing from the wound.

Elise walked in the door.

She had shot him?

Then he saw the bigger man behind her. In a haze of pain he saw her being herded toward him by a man they'd all thought was dead.

Tucker stepped forward. "Zane—"

The man behind Elise lifted his gun and shot Tucker.

Elise ran to a hurt Jonah before Zane could stop her. She pulled off her sweater and pressed it against Jonah's wound, tying the arms around his leg. She whimpered, making a point not to look at the dead man on the floor only a few paces from them.

Jonah gritted his teeth against the pain. "Sorry."

Jonah grunted, but she could only think how he wouldn't be mixed up in this if it wasn't for her. He'd stuck around, making a point to step in and end it because of her. "I'm so sorry."

"Not your fault." He bit the words out, and Elise's heart turned over.

She glanced back at Zane Ford, the former zookeeper. "How could you do this? You're supposed to care for animals, how can you sell them like this? Given to people who, at best, have no clue the extent of how to care for them, and at worst will mistreat them in unimaginable ways."

She'd known Zane Ford before, years ago when she was a youth volunteer at the zoo, and he'd never had that hard, dead look in his eyes back then. He'd cared for the animals, and though he'd been aloof, she'd attributed that to the fact that he'd been in charge.

"You think I wanted to waste my life in a worthless excuse for a zoo? It's hardly big enough for more than a few goats and that old tiger." He waved his arm at the tiger. The shotgun had been discarded in the grass on the way over to the barn in favor of a handgun. Both were scary enough.

"Please." Zane shook his head. "I have plans, and plans require cold hard cash I won't get on city pay doing fund-raisers and schmoozing

with small-town bigwigs, begging for money to pay for animal feed and basic repairs."

Elise glanced at Jonah. His eyes were open, and he mouthed, *Are you okay?*

She blinked in affirmation while Zane kept talking. "This way there's a whole lot less stink to shovel around. I deliver, and I get paid."

Elise wanted to throw up. She wanted to scream at Zane, but she kept her eyes on Jonah and not the crazy man still yelling, or the dead guy across the barn. She looked at the man she loved, bleeding out on the floor and mouthed, *Parker.*

Jonah's brow flickered for a second.

Elise mouthed, *Outside.*

Jonah needed hope, and the chance that Parker might have seen or heard Zane take her from Jonah's barn just might be enough to get them through this. Jonah knew Parker had been with her, and if anyone could track a missing person it should be a former SEAL. Right?

Zane had only dragged her across the field to Jonah's neighbor's barn. It was a couple of miles easy, but that was close in country like this.

It shouldn't take Parker long to find them.

Jonah's gaze caught hers again. "Run." The word was a breathy whisper. "Run, Elise."

That was the second time tonight someone

had told her to run. She looked at the only door, where Zane blocked the way with his loaded gun. Stairs in the opposite corner led up to a loft. Was there a window up there? It wouldn't be the first time tonight she'd jumped. Could she chance—again—not breaking her leg? Jonah certainly couldn't go, though. And she wasn't likely to leave him here to die. So that idea was out.

Besides, Jonah's teammate should be here, as soon as he was done helping Hailey. Elise didn't know how to communicate that Parker might be two minutes, or ten. Taking a breath, Elise mouthed, *Pray.*

Jonah immediately nodded. She'd heard him pray earlier, but it still surprised Elise. She was glad he was willing to trust God with the outcome of tonight. She hadn't stopped praying since Jonah left, since he gave her that kiss that changed everything.

Zane grabbed her arm and dragged her to her feet. She swung around fighting, despite the fact that he had a gun. Elise was done with this. She was ready to get out of here, and if she could help it, then she was going to do everything in her power. Zane whipped up the gun and slammed it into her temple before she could get her head out of the way.

Elise dropped to her knees, stars in front of

her eyes. She blinked and blinked. Even so it took minutes before she could see again.

"Elise." It was Jonah. "Elise!"

She chanced a look at Jonah, which hurt. Fear for her was in his eyes. He'd sat up, looking like he was getting ready to come over to her.

"No. Stay there." He shouldn't move, not with a wound.

The sound of an engine firing brought her attention around the other direction. Fix's truck pulled out, spewing gravel and exhaust fumes into the barn. Zane parked, and a door slammed before he got into a different vehicle and backed it up to Fix's trailer.

Elise couldn't let him get the animals. She wasn't going to let him take them and sell them. He was done with his evil business.

Elise climbed to her feet and stumbled to the trailer. She reached in and found Shera's cage. With a flip of the latches she opened each in turn, leaving the door shut so the animal would only have to push the door open to get out. She looked Shera in the eye and motioned for her to come, praying the nearly blind feline would see something.

But Zane was done hooking his vehicle to the trailer. "What are you doing?"

She spun. "Checking the animals. That's all. Just making sure they're okay."

"Your concern is not required. You think I don't know they're fine? Look at them." He motioned to the truck even while he kept the gun trained on her. "They're ready to go meet their new owners, and there's nothing you can do about it."

Zane disappeared again, and Elise hopped out of the trailer. She looked for something to hit the man with, maybe try and knock him out, but there was nothing. And then he was back.

Zane set a can of gasoline on the floor inside the door. "Time to finish this."

Elise crouched by Jonah while Zane flicked the can around the room, spraying gas on dry straw, on wooden beams and all over the walls.

She pulled up on Jonah's arms and he got the message, gritted his teeth and started to get up. Elise swung his arm across her shoulder, helping him to stand. Like a team, the way they'd always been.

"You can't leave us here to die," Jonah said. She could hear the pain in his voice, but didn't think Zane would notice. Or care. "Conspiracy to kill the reporter is different than committing murder yourself now. You're throwing away the rest of your life. You won't be able to walk away from this."

Zane huffed, pulling out a lighter. "That's where you're wrong. I'm the only one who gets to walk away from this."

Elise chanced a look to the side. Shera climbed silently from the trailer, her steps muffled on the earthy floor. Shera turned her head side to side, disoriented from the pervading smell of gasoline. Elise had to distract Zane for a second, so she yelled, "Don't do this! We don't want to die!" with all the hysteria she was feeling, allowing the fear to infuse every part of her.

Zane grinned, an awful evil smile. He flicked the top off the lighter and struck a flame. Shera was still, apparently unsure of where to go.

Zane was going to toss it on the gasoline, and they were going to die.

NINETEEN

Zane's gaze flickered to Shera. His eyes widened and he dropped the flip-top lighter, the flame staying steady as it fell to the floor. Seizing the opportunity, Jonah ignored the pain in his leg and ran to the former zookeeper. He slammed into Zane and they hit the ground. Zane's gun went off.

Jonah delivered punch after punch, putting every ounce of rage at the pain he and Elise had suffered because of Zane's selfish actions, trying to make money by any means necessary.

Elise screamed, Sam started barking and the room filled with smoke.

Jonah looked up just as his dog ran in. Parker appeared at the door. "Rivers!" About to enter, Parker's eyes widened at the scene in the barn.

Fire rushed across the wall, whipped into a frenzy, trying to reach the air at the open door. Flames licked across the entry, cutting off Parker's attempt to enter.

"Stay back!" He didn't think the order would stop Parker from trying to get in and help them, but it was worth a try.

"Jonah!"

He turned to Elise. The last place she needed to be was in a barn that was now on fire. He coughed into his elbow and turned to Sam. "Guard."

The dog set his paws on an unconscious Zane Ford.

Jonah scrambled to Elise, who was leaning over Shera. "What happened?"

Elise's hands pressed into the tiger's side. "Zane's gun. He shot her." She sucked in a choppy breath. "I don't know what to do. She needs help!"

And so do we. Jonah ran his hand up and down her back. "We'll get her help. But first, we have to get out of here."

The animals in the trailer were starting to screech and scream at the smoke. The air was hot with no relief, and smoke was choking his lungs. *God, help us.*

Gears on the truck shifted, and it was pulled out of the entrance to the barn, dragging the trailer. Parker. As soon as he cleared the doorway, Jonah breathed a sigh of relief. "Let's go."

He was getting Elise out of there, and then

he'd figure out with Parker how to haul a four-hundred-pound shot tiger out of the barn. And Zane.

They reached the door, Sam's eyes on them. The barn wall creaked, and with a mighty crack the roof above the front door came down.

Jonah stumbled to a stop while Elise screamed. Flames jumped around, and they had to move back. He looked around. They were surrounded now by a wall of flames penning them in.

"How are we going to get out now?" Elise had to shout over the roar of flames.

Parker's voice came from far away, "I already called the fire department."

At least that was something. Provided they could hold on long enough for firefighters to get them out and get the fire contained.

He looked around again. The loft was still standing, on the opposite side from the door, but they'd have to drag everyone up the stairs. He looked from the loft to the tiger, to the man lying unconscious.

"We need a way out…"

Elise shook her head. "There was only one door."

Jonah went to Shera and knelt by the tiger. He pushed with all his remaining strength and moved the tiger more toward the center of the room. Shera grunted and shifted. He patted her neck, knowing she was confused and unable to see the predicament they were in. At least she was away from the flames now.

Elise stood in the center of the room.

"We can't go up, since we can't carry everyone up the stairs." His brain worked the problem, his eyes scanning the floor. "So if we can't go up, or out, we'll have to go down."

"Into the floor?"

"Maybe there's a cellar of some kind. Help me look."

They searched every inch of floor until Jonah found the latch. He couldn't get it open with his fingers, so he kicked at it with his boot. When that didn't work, he got Zane's gun and hammered at the latch with the butt of the gun.

When it broke off, he pulled up the opening, revealing a small cellar dug out of the dirt. Jonah didn't know what Tucker had kept down there, and neither did he want to find out.

"How do we get Shera down there?"

Jonah shook his head. Zane was still out, so he said, "Sam. Come." The dog trotted over. Jonah clicked his fingers and Sam went down the steps, turning in the six-foot-by-six-foot space before sitting down.

Jonah looked at Elise. "Help me. She's so heavy that we're going to drop her. We will just have to help her get down as easily as we can."

"Okay. Tell me what to do."

Jonah squeezed her hand. Together they pushed Shera to the cellar entrance. Jonah went down first and Elise came down beside him. They maneuvered the tiger over the hole and guided her down to the floor as slow as they could. The weight was massive. Jonah's leg buckled, and Shera hit the floor. The tiger growled, and Elise crouched. "Sorry, Shera."

Then she looked at him. "You okay?"

Jonah nodded even though his leg felt like it was on fire. "I have to go back for Zane."

"Why? He tried to kill us!" Hurt filled Elise's eyes. "Why save him?"

"He has to face justice, or what's the point? He needs to be alive so he can see what he did was wrong. So he can pay."

Jonah climbed the stairs, even though his leg blatantly wanted him to stay put. But so long as Elise stayed safe with the animals, he was good. Air was better down there, and the dirt made it cooler.

Jonah grabbed Zane's feet and dragged him to the cellar. He wanted the man alive, but didn't much care how many bruises he had, not considering how many injuries Zane had given Elise over the past few days.

Jonah pulled him to the entrance and rolled him down the four short steps to tumble on the floor at the bottom. Then he climbed down after him and closed the door.

Jonah made it to the wall and leaned so his back was against the cool earth. Smoke laced the air down here now, and he could hear Sam and Elise moving around.

He opened his eyes and glanced at her. Sam had settled his head on her leg, which made Jonah smile even while his heart was racing and he wondered how long they were going to be stuck down there.

Elise's lips were moving. Jonah shook his head, he couldn't hear her.

She frowned and started to move toward him, but Jonah held her off. There wasn't enough room for her to make her way over to him.

Jonah felt himself slide to the side. If he kept going, he'd end up beside Shera. He tried to keep himself upright, but couldn't lift his shoulders. Jonah looked at his leg, pooling blood on the floor.

He slid sideways more, pain slicing through his leg as his body twisted.

Elise screamed.

Jonah's world went black.

Elise watched Jonah slip into unconsciousness. The pain was obviously great, and he'd exerted himself far beyond what he should have when the bullet had cut all the way through his leg. He needed serious medical treatment, Shera needed a vet and they had to get out of there.

The building above them was on fire. The cellar was protecting them, but it was only slowing down the attack of flames. Eventually they were going to be burned alive.

Elise choked back a sob. God wasn't supposed to take any more from her. That wasn't the deal they'd made when she became a Christian. She could do this, so long as she didn't lose anyone else. The guilt and grief over Martin's death had swallowed her, and the only reason she'd stayed sane was because she'd had Nathan.

Now she was alone with two unconscious men, Jonah and Shera were dying, and Sam looked like he'd retreated to some place in his head instead of being here to experience what was going on.

Thank God Jonah was still breathing. How was she going to survive him dying? It had been hard enough to lose him when he was still alive and there was a glimmer of hope that one day she would see him again. There was no way they had a future if he was killed tonight.

Tears tracked down her face, and she couldn't help remembering the Bible verses she'd memorized over the years. The ones about peace and hope, a future. But where was that hope now?

God, You can't let me down now. They'd come so far and He'd held her up all these years on her own as a mom. *Help us, please. Don't let Jonah die here in a dirty cellar, so close to help. Don't let us die.*

Elise wanted to tell Bernadette that she forgave her. For everything.

Life was too fragile to let someone continue holding the guilt of what they'd done. Not if Elise could do something to alleviate that guilt. Bernadette needed to know it was okay for her to have a fresh start of her own. Especially when that was exactly what Elise had been given.

She only had one thing she hadn't done yet. The real reason she'd come home—to visit Martin's grave and finally tell him she was sorry. She didn't deserve to have her guilt alleviated, not considering how selfish she'd been. But it was the only way she was going to be able to move on, to find that future with Jonah she prayed they both wanted.

For the first time since coming home, Elise was glad that God had brought her back to town. Even if it had started because Bernadette wanted to make amends with Elise and get to know Nathan. Elise was glad God had given her this second chance with Jonah.

Please don't take it away now. Not when it finally might be possible.

Zane groaned. Elise's eyes darted to him in time to watch him shift and open his eyes.

She coughed against the smoke getting thicker by the minute. Zane pressed his hands against the floor and lifted up. Water poured in the crack around the cellar door. It dripped down the steps and hit Jonah's good leg first.

Zane blinked, his gaze zeroing on her first.

She coughed again, barely able to see across the small space.

"You did this!" He shifted toward her but stalled as though he didn't have the energy to fulfill his intention. "This is your fault!"

"I'm not the one selling animals, and I'm not the one who set the fire."

Fear and anxiety had distilled. There was nothing in Elise but pure anger at Zane Ford for his selfishness in bringing them all together to die.

God, please don't let us go out like this.

Water was still pouring down the steps. Hopefully the firefighters would reach them, find them, soon.

Zane rose to sit, then crawled to her. His eyes were on fire with rage, making her stomach churn. She pulled up her feet, knees to her chest. Was he going to—

He climbed over Shera, unconcerned for the animal's comfort.

Sam twitched and rose to sit, his eyes on Ford.

Elise said, "What are you doing?"

He kept coming. When he was close enough to her, he reached out. Elise tried to fight him off with her hands, but he got close enough to wrap his big fingers around her throat. She batted at his forearms even as he began to squeeze. They were minutes from death by smoke inhalation. What was he doing?

"I told you that you were going to die."

She gasped for breath but couldn't get air. Zane kept squeezing and the little oxygen she got in her lungs was more smoke than air.

A noise emerged from her throat, high and feral, as she fought him. She added her legs, kicking against him until he pressed down on her legs to keep her still.

Sam barked.

Overhead, Elise heard multiple pairs of boots moving around, like they were frantically searching. She fought harder, trying to make more noise.

We're down here.

Sparks lit the edges of her vision as she lost

the ability to breathe, her windpipe closing. Sam's jaw led his attack, clamping down on Zane's arm. His grip slipped, and Elise tried to suck in air. She coughed, her lungs and throat on fire, and started to slip sideways toward the floor just as Jonah had done.

Zane cried out, trying to get Sam off him.

The dog yelped.

Elise tried to move, but her limbs were leaden.

The door above them was pulled open and a rush of heat made the air even thicker. Flames burned bright up in the barn.

Someone said, "Hurry up. The whole place is about to come down."

TWENTY

Jonah woke with a plastic oxygen mask over his face. The air filling his lungs smelled cold, and goose bumps rose on his forearms. The lights in the ambulance were bright, the doors open and the world outside a bustle of lights, noise and people.

He shifted to sit, and a hand pressed against his shoulder. Hailey Shelder shifted into view. "Hold up, boss."

He blinked, trying to figure out why she had butterfly bandages across her cheek.

"Don't get up." She grinned. "The EMTs will get mad at me if you do that. Your leg…" She motioned to it and grimaced.

Right. His leg. Although he couldn't really feel it. Or much of anything. Probably because of the tube attached to his arm. Jonah looked around, but no one else was in their vicinity, so he lifted himself up on the unencumbered elbow. Where was Elise? How had they gotten out? Was Zane in custody?

Hailey had her jacket off, revealing a bandage around her left arm. She rolled her eyes. "He only winged me. You'd think it was serious the way Eric is carrying on."

Jonah knew exactly why the man was acting like that. Over the past few days he'd gained a fresh respect for Eric, having his woman be constantly in the line of fire.

"You agree with him." She scowled at Jonah. "Traitor. You're supposed to be sticking up for me, telling my fiancé how I'm so capable at my job, I can accept the risks so he can, too."

Jonah shot her a look.

"Like I said. Traitor."

He pulled the mask down.

"You're supposed to keep that on. Smoke inhalation."

He didn't replace it. "Where's—"

"Eric should be back in a minute. Thankfully we got a breather from him being all intense and protecty, but he had to cover for Parker and get Zane squared away with the cops."

"Done and done." Eric climbed into the ambulance. He sat beside Hailey and brushed hair from her shoulder, down her back.

Jonah lay back down, unable to continue holding himself up on his elbow.

Hailey said, "Zane is in custody?"

"Took him to the hospital first to get checked out, and then he'll go on to be booked. He'd have been facing attempted murder, anyway. Parker went with him, to get his hands treated."

"What's wrong with his hands?" Hailey frowned. "I didn't see him after he came back to help me." She glanced at Jonah. "Zane's bullet hit my arm, and wood from the door shattering cut my cheek, but Zane had gone out the door. I called emergency and when Parker came in your house, I sent him back to help Elise. I waited for the ambulance and cops, and after a while we saw the commotion at Tucker's barn. And the smoke."

Eric looked at Jonah. "I waited with Hailey, who was getting treated, and Parker called in from Tucker's. After he pulled the truck and trailer out he burned his hands trying to get to you guys." He paused. "Parker feels real bad you all were in there so long."

Jonah said, "How bad are the burns?"

"Second degree, the EMT said. But he'll be back, fighting fit in no time. You'll see." He slipped his arm around Hailey and sighed. "I don't get why Zane needed to try and strangle Elise when it was already over for him."

Hailey made an affirmative noise, even while

Jonah pulled his mask down again. "What did you say?"

Eric frowned. "He strangled her."

Hailey glanced at Eric, then said, "She's okay. It was right when the firefighters pulled you guys out. She's been treated already, and Nathan is here. Ames brought him from the office where Parker had stashed him during the operation. Your mom is here, too. I saw her. And the mayor. Everyone's okay."

Okay was fine, but Jonah wanted to see Elise for himself. "Where is she now?"

Eric waved toward the door. "Around, somewhere. Firefighters pulled Tucker's body out. Looks like your neighbor was up to his neck in this."

He'd thought Tucker was a brother, a fellow vet enjoying retirement after serving his country. Not a criminal entrenched in illegal animal trading.

Jonah looked out the door again, anxious to see Elise and know for himself she was finally out of harm's way. Then he turned back to Eric and Hailey. "How about Shera? She was shot. How is she now?"

Eric said, "Shera was taken to the closest vet. Rushed into surgery, the last I heard. You should have seen the firefighters all hanging around." He grinned. "Once they figured out she wasn't a threat, they all wanted to pet her, and be the one to ride with her to the doctor. Funniest thing I've ever seen."

"And Sam?" Jonah said. "He was down there, too."

Hailey smiled. "Took to Elise. Won't leave her side, no matter what anyone tries to do. It's why she couldn't—and didn't want to—go to the hospital. EMTs cleared her, since her throat was just bruised. Everything else was bumps, scratches and old injuries already treated. She's had a seriously rough few days. I don't envy her the time it's going to take to heal from all this. But she's got Sam now. He seems to have appointed himself as her official protector."

Jonah was glad she had Sam, but he still wanted to see her. "Maybe you could go find—"

"Rivers!" Detective William Manners rocked back and forth on his shoes, just outside the ambulance doors. "Glad to see you're awake." He glanced back, toward where the smoke still lingered around the barn. "Some kind of thing, eh? Never seen the like, hiding in a barn cellar, tiger with a gunshot wound. Wouldn't have believed it if you'd told me."

Jonah didn't know what to say, so he lay back again. Where was Elise?

"Anyway, ballistics report came back on the bullet that killed the reporter, and the one that destroyed your mailbox—found that in the grass. Both of them trace back to purchases made by your neighbor. Looks like Tucker was behind the reporter's death, and the attempts on your girl's life."

Maybe, but where was she?

"You just concentrate on getting that leg all healed up." The detective grinned. "I'll worry about cleanup over here, and at your place."

So Manners had made the arrests, while Jonah had been injured and personally detained no one? It wasn't a competition between departments, but that wasn't the point. Cops would get all the credit, and Jonah would only have what he'd got into it for—Fix Tanner in custody.

He glanced at the detective. "Great. Glad to hear you'll cover all the paperwork."

Detective Manners sputtered, his face reddening. "Of course not. What do I look like, the maid?" He motioned a meaty finger at Jonah's leg. "You heal up quick, now. There's plenty of paperwork and meetings to go around."

Jonah nodded. "I'm sure there is."

Where on earth was Elise? Wasn't she concerned about him? Surely she'd have been over by now if she was, instead of ignoring his ambulance and staying completely out of sight so other people could tell him how "okay" she was.

The woman had been nearly suffocated, burned and strangled. She'd likely had about as much as she could take. But it was over now.

"Well, I'll leave you to it." Manners gave them a wave and strode away.

"You'll be heading out soon. I expect," Eric said. "I should get out and tell the EMTs you're ready for transport. Get that leg looked at, yeah?"

Speaking of which... Jonah clenched his stomach and sat up straight.

"No—"

He shot Hailey a look and she held back what she'd been about to say. He moved his good leg off the bed and tested it against some weight.

"This isn't a good idea." Eric held up his hands. "Just tell me what you need."

Sweat beaded on Jonah's brow. "Get Elise in here. Now. No more waiting."

Eric said, "I'll find her, okay? Just lie back down. I'm sure Elise is somewhere around—"

"I'm right here."

Elise bit her lip, feeling her son close in to her side. She knew she looked bad, but Jonah was the one lying on the ambulance bed. "We should be quick. You need to go to the hospital and have your leg seen to."

He just held out his hand to her.

Eric climbed out. "I'm going to go talk to the EMTs. Find out when you're going to be treated."

Elise climbed in. "Aren't you bleeding everywhere?" They'd only been out of the barn maybe ten minutes, but still. Shouldn't he have been taken to the hospital by now?

She glanced back at Sam, who'd been pressed to her side since the cellar. He sat at the door, eyes on her and Jonah.

Hailey was the one who answered. "They wrapped his leg. Now I think they were waiting to see if anyone else needed to go. This is the only available ambulance left in the county, since there was a crash on the highway."

"Oh." Elise stopped, not sure if she was supposed to sit by Hailey, or by Jonah.

Hailey pulled her down to her side, then got up. "I'm going to go help Eric."

With her gone, they were alone, save for Sam. Nathan had disappeared.

"How is Nathan?"

She glanced at Jonah. "He's okay. It was a rough night, not knowing if we were okay when he was totally fine. Both of us are glad it's over."

Because it was. Over.

He said, "How are you?"

She surveyed him. Jonah's face was pale, a sheen of sweat on his hairline. "I feel better than you look."

Despite the bruises on her neck, she was okay. Nothing that sleep and a couple weeks of aches wouldn't cure. He'd been shot.

Jonah chuckled, then groaned. But he didn't lie down. He just sat there, his steel-gray eyes dark and focused on her.

"I'm exhausted, truth be told." Elise sighed. "And gross."

She badly needed a shower. Probably two just to get the smell of smoke out.

"I don't think you've ever looked more beautiful."

Elise laughed. "Not even the time we were in Canon Beach when I fell in that puddle and I was covered in mud?"

Jonah's lips curled up into a genuine smile. "Not even."

Sure, she'd been a child then. But it wasn't like she looked like a movie star now. She was just a regular woman. Why did he think she was beautiful? He'd never even seen her made-up, ready to go out. Dressed nice, like in that yellow dress her friend had given her and she'd never worn.

"What is it?"

Elise shrugged. What was she supposed to

say? Jonah had been shot because of her. He was going to have to take time off work because of her. Never before had he tolerated her holding him back from what he wanted to do. He'd always done what he had to and put her off until later.

Now all she could think of were the million reasons he had to do it again. What if, now that there was no reason to put a hold on their relationship, Jonah decided he didn't want her?

His hand came up, his fingers touching her cheek so gently that she lifted her face. Elise looked at him through the sheen of tears.

Jonah's hand left her face, and then he reacted. "Soot on your cheek. Sorry."

She swiped at her face, probably making it worse. But who cared? They both already knew she was nothing special. "It's fine."

"Why does it feel like you're pulling away?"

Elise shrugged. "I have a lot to do, and you need to get to the hospital. Eric will be back any minute. You should go with him and Hailey. Get checked out. You probably need stitches, or surgery——" Her voice broke then.

"Elise, I'm fine." He chuckled. "Okay, not totally fine, but I will be. I'll heal. But my heart won't, not if you leave me like this, Elise."

She blinked. "What?"

"I'm in love with you."

She stared at him. He was going to do this *now*?

"I want a chance with you. I know you're not about to up and leave town again, but I feel like if I don't tell you now, then I'll never get the chance. You ever feel like that? Like life is going to slip out of your fingers and you'll never get it back?"

She nodded.

"So what do you say, Elise? You and me, forever?"

She squeezed her eyes shut, overwhelmed with the fact that she'd just been given everything she had always wanted. Nathan had been a blessing she'd never known she wanted, or needed. Jonah, a future with him... *Forever*. It was like finding the gold at the end of a rainbow.

She opened her eyes. "I do love you. That was never the problem."

"So, then, what—"

Nathan knocked on the back door of the ambulance, like they were in an office meeting. "I'm heading out to check on Shera. I'll take Sam with me, since he can't go to the hospital. I can call, keep you posted on the tiger's condition if you want."

Elise shook her head. "I'm coming with you."

"Elise—"

She slipped from Jonah's grasp before he could reach for her, and stumbled to the end of the ambulance, trying not to cry. Not yet. When she was alone was a different story, but Jonah didn't need to see the affect he had on her.

"Mom, are you sure? You don't need to come."

"Sure I do. I'm the zookeeper now. One of my animals is hurt, and I should be there to make sure she's going to pull through."

Sam nudged her hand, making the lump in her throat thicken. She was going to choke on it if she didn't get out of there.

Jonah might say he loved her, but that was because he hadn't processed fully what had happened yet. When he did that, he was going to realize she wasn't worth the trouble. And Elise had no intention of still being around when that happened. Talk about uncomfortable and embarrassing. There was no way she wanted to see it. Or to hear him apologize. Or see the sorry look in his eyes.

There was no way.

"Elise—"

She didn't look back at Jonah. He thought he wanted her there, but that was because he was pale and in shock. He'd lost blood all over the cellar floor. A pool of it.

An EMT brushed past her and shut the doors on Jonah, who was still calling out for her.

He needed to go to hospital, not to be stuck there, talking to her. He didn't even know what he was saying, did he? He couldn't. Otherwise he'd know she wasn't the answer to his problems.

Some people just weren't meant to be.

TWENTY-ONE

Jonah hit the button to raise the hospital bed. Soon as the nurse got back with crutches and his paperwork, he was out of there. Back to his empty house with not even his own dog to keep him company.

Unless he did something about it.

He'd thought they had an understanding, but evidently Elise didn't know that. Jonah didn't get how it was possible, given that he'd made his feelings pretty clear. So, what was holding her back? If Martin was alive, it might have been a different story. But he'd died a long time ago.

Whatever was in Elise's head that was stopping her from fully connecting with him might have been there for a long, long time. Maybe even back to the day he left and joined the marines.

The door handle shifted. Then again. Then someone thumped the door. Finally it opened.

Parker's face was red from struggling with the door, and his hands were bandaged.

"Hey. How are you doing?"

Parker growled. "Can't even get a stupid door open, how do you think I'm doing?"

Jonah bit back a grin. "You'll be healed up in no time, I'm sure."

"I better be."

"So, what's up? I'm leaving in a minute."

"Back to the office?"

Jonah shook his head. "Got somewhere to be."

"Oh. Right. I'll be fast, then." Parker didn't look like he agreed with what Jonah was doing, but given his opinion on women in general, that wasn't unexpected. Someone had broken his teammate's heart, and it was going to take a God-style intervention to put the pieces back together.

Parker opened his mouth again, and Ames strode in the door. Parker grimaced. "Dude, where were you two minutes ago?"

"Talking to the nurse." Ames grinned. "What of it? Just looking out for my boy here, getting an update."

"Sure you were." Jonah laughed. He was the opposite of Parker, but Jonah figured that didn't necessarily mean Ames didn't also have a broken heart. He was just better at hiding it.

Jonah glanced at Parker. "You wanna sit?"

His teammate nodded. "So it turns out that the reporter did an article six months back about your neighbor, Tucker. About what a shining example he was of being a vet, retired, giving back to the community. Probably followed him around for days. We figure that's how the reporter first worked out that Tucker was up to something, because of the assignment, and why he was in the zoo office, when Elise found and spooked him."

Jonah could see how that might've happened. "So Tucker gets wind of the reporter still being in his business. Or Zane realizes someone's poking around, and they go after the reporter."

Parker said, "PD thinks Tucker is the one who planted that bomb in the zoo office. Trying to destroy evidence and kill the reporter at the same time."

"And then they decided to kill Elise since they figured she knew, or she'd find evidence they might've missed."

Ames leaned against the wall, arms folded. "Zane must have decided to use the flood to fake his death, figuring everyone would assume he was lost in the storm and his body simply washed away. Used the cover of the flood to move his business out of state, until it started to get out and he realized there were still loose ends to tie up. Maybe he was planning all along to kill Tucker before he left town."

Jonah was seriously glad it was over. Elise was finally safe, finally able to start her life here in town. A life that hopefully was going to include him.

"Over now."

Jonah nodded at Parker's sage reply. "Sure is."

"So where is she?" Ames glanced around, like Elise might've been hiding behind a curtain.

Jonah didn't give them the satisfaction of looking discomfited by the question. "She went to check on Shera with Nathan. Sam wasn't going to be able to come here, so he's with her, too."

Parker and Ames exchanged a look.

"Okay, fine." Jonah folded his arms. "What do I do about Elise?"

Ames said, "Because you're recovering from your valiant attempt to save your woman from the people trying to kill her, and she's somewhere else? Not here, showing you just how grateful she is?"

"She's grateful. I think she's just also… scared."

"Makes sense." Ames nodded. "Your brother died. She probably doesn't want a repeat of that."

"As soon as the nurse gets back with my crutches and the paperwork, I'm going to find her."

"But if you don't know how to address her fears, it's not going to be worth much."

Parker shook his head. "They're her fears. Jonah can't bend over backward trying to solve a problem she has to come to terms with on her own."

Ames said, "How long will that take? He's waited nearly twenty years. You want him to wait even longer?"

"He might have to if there's nothing he can do. She might have to get past this on her own, or not at all." He turned to Jonah. "It's been a long, harrowing weekend for her. Maybe you need to give her space for a little longer."

"But—"

"Okay, okay." Jonah held up both hands.

The sense of urgency still hadn't left him. *God, I can't even get up and walk to her myself. Can't the nurse hurry up? Otherwise I'm stuck with these two and they'll probably launch into another argument.*

It was so much more natural now to reach out to God. He was Lord of Elise's life, and Jonah wanted that same relationship with God from now on.

The nurse walked in, pushing a wheelchair, followed by an aide carrying crutches.

"Great." Jonah moved to hop off the bed.

The nurse's eyebrow rose. "Somewhere you need to be, Marshal?"

Ames grinned. "My boy's got a hot date with the woman of his dreams."

The nurse's eyes turned wistful for a second; then she smiled. "Good for you."

"I'd ask your advice, but I think I already figured out what I need to do to persuade her she should say yes to me." He took two steps on the crutches and then turned back to his two teammates, motioning to the door. "I need a ride. Let's go."

Ames grinned. "I guess we're coming with you."

Parker pushed the wheelchair and waited with Jonah while Ames pulled the SUV around. By the time Jonah was buckled in the back-seat, there was yet another sheen of sweat on his upper body.

Ames turned around. "Where to, sir?"

Jonah rattled off his mom's address. "To start with."

Ames pulled away from the curb while Jonah took his phone out and dialed his mom's number.

She answered on the second ring. "Darling,

how are you?" The concern in her voice was genuine, and made him feel better about what he was going to ask her for.

Since he couldn't lie and say he was fine, Jonah said, "Don't go anywhere. I'll be there in ten minutes."

"Still nothing?"

Nathan slumped into the chair next to her. "Still nothing."

Shera was still in surgery, but what did it mean that it was taking so long? A gunshot wound was complicated to repair whether it was a person or a tiger. Still, it was pretty uncommon for a vet to deal with. She prayed this one was competent enough, and Shera wasn't past the point where she had enough strength for her big body to aid the healing process.

Nathan reached over and took her hand. "You okay?"

Elise shrugged. She wasn't about to lie to him.

"I'm sorry I interrupted whatever that was between you and Uncle Jonah. I should've waited, but our ride was pretty anxious to leave."

"It's okay."

"Is it?"

She shifted her body in the chair to look at

him. Sam didn't lift his head from her leg, and he didn't open his eyes. "Why are you asking me that?"

"It's pretty obvious how he feels about you," Nathan said. "If I hadn't heard him say it, I could have told you that by the look on his face when you walked away."

He paused a moment, long enough for Elise to wonder why he was doing this. Then Nathan continued. "I want to know why you're not jumping at the chance to have a relationship with him. I want to know why you're going to let this opportunity pass by without at least trying, let alone fighting for something you want. I've seen you do it, when it's an animal not receiving the proper care, or someone treating them like their lives aren't worth anything. Why won't you do that for yourself?"

She shook her head. "You don't understand. It isn't like that."

"Isn't it? I think you're scared, but you know that it could be great. It could. You could be actually happy—"

"You think I'm not happy?"

"You are. To an extent. But I know there's more you want. And I want to go to college knowing there's someone here to spend time with you, to take care of you. Not that you can't take care of yourself. I know you can. But I don't want you to be alone, Mom."

Elise bit her lip. She didn't want to be alone, either, and she'd felt that way for a very long time. Having a child was a fulfilling experience, but it didn't give the satisfaction a romantic relationship did. That a marriage would—to Jonah. She couldn't think of anyone else she'd want to be married to. There was only him, there always had been and there always would be.

Could she let go of what was holding her back and finally seize what God had put in front of her—the chance to have what she had always wanted and never believed she would ever have again?

The door opened, got stuck and commotion brought her attention around as someone struggled to get in on crutches.

Elise jumped up. "Jonah?"

She ran to hold the door open, alarmed at the way he looked. He grimaced with each step. His eyes had lines and dark circles of exhaustion and he wasn't any less pale than he'd been in the ambulance.

"Did they even help you at the hospital? You don't look much better at all."

He sat on the chair beside where she'd been, easing down slowly before he pushed out a breath between pursed lips. "Sewed me up. Gave me medicine."

"Is it wearing off?"

He looked at his watch. "Can't take more for an hour."

Elise looked over at Nathan, sharing her concern with her glance. Nathan stood, squeezing her elbow as he passed. "I'm going to go check with the nurse again."

Elise sat, and Jonah reached for her hand. With his other, he scratched Sam's head while the dog licked his wrist.

She smiled at him. "You really don't look well."

"I'm well enough for this. But I might need a nap later." Jonah lifted the back of her hand to his lips.

She allowed the sensation to wash through her, wondering that it was his presence that gave her the strength to overcome her fears. *Thank You, God, for that gift.*

"I—"

"Elise—"

They both smiled. He said, "Let me go first, please." When she nodded, he continued. "I've always loved you, Elise. You know that."

She nodded. He'd told her, and more than proven it over the past few days.

"What I need to know is how you feel about

me. Not years ago, but now. Today." His eyes searched her face. "Do you love me?"

Elise took a breath, praying for yet more strength. "Of course I do."

Jonah didn't respond. He reached into his pocket and pulled out a tiny velvet bag. "I got this from my mom."

"When?"

He grinned. "About ten minutes ago."

Elise laughed.

He tipped the contents of the bag and held up a gorgeous antique diamond ring that would look ridiculous on her finger while she tended to dirty, smelly zoo animals.

"If you don't like it—"

Elise stilled his hand. "I love it."

His mother had given him what was clearly a family heirloom. Years ago Bernadette hadn't gifted Martin with the ring to give to Elise, but she had given it to Jonah.

Elise didn't need flashy things, but she thanked God for Bernadette's acceptance of her. She didn't deserve it, but it was a gift she would relish, anyway.

Nathan was right. She had to get past the fear and open her heart to Jonah.

She said, "There's just one thing missing."

"What's that?"

"You actually have to ask the question."

"Oh." He blushed. "Right. Well, what do you say? Will you marry me, Elise?"

Fresh laughter bubbled up. "Are you even going to remember this when you come down off whatever pain medication they have you on?"

He looked aghast. "You think I'm going to forget?" He slung his arm around her shoulder. "Put me out of my misery, woman."

"Yes."

The answer didn't take away the fear, but she had a lifetime with Jonah for God to prove Himself faithful to her—to them.

"When? I don't want to wait."

Elise smiled. "I don't want to wait, either."

"Big or small ceremony?"

"Do you think we can have a small ceremony in your mom's garden?"

Jonah kissed her hand again. "I think she would love that."

Since he looked like he was about to fall over, Elise snuggled closer, turning her face up to him so he could read there exactly what she wanted.

Jonah leaned in, covering her mouth with his in a kiss that swept her away and promised wonderful things about their future.

When he pulled back, his eyes went to the hall beyond them. "Sorry."

Elise looked over in time to see Nathan shrug. "It's gross, but whatever." He looked at her. "Shera's out of surgery. She's going to be fine."

Elise's heart overflowed with happiness. She'd come home to find a future for Nathan, where he could reach for his dreams and she could help him to do that without being tied down with student loans and guilt for leaving her.

Instead, God had given her everything she wanted. Her long-buried dreams for her future had come to light, and in the midst of her fear He'd given her the strength to rise above it and accept everything He'd offered her.

Thank You, Lord.

EPILOGUE

Three months later, Elise stared at the headstone, her gaze tracing the letters of Martin's name.

"I'm sorry." She hung her head, trying to keep her composure, considering that her new husband and her son were probably watching her from the car. But she needed to do this.

"I wasn't what you deserved, and I didn't really try and be the wife you needed. Eventually you gave up trying to make me love you, and you went off to please your brother by doing something he'd be proud of instead."

Bernadette took her hand, gently squeezing it. Elise didn't look over at her mother-in-law; she simply listened while Bernadette said, "Martin, we all could have done better by you. So much life, so much drive. You didn't always apply it in a good way, but we didn't try and help you with that, either. You knew your mind, and you stuck with it."

Bernadette sucked in a breath. "You will always hold a special place in our hearts. And you have our promise that we will help your son figure out how to be the man we always knew you could be. Because that's what you gave to him. And we're so grateful for it."

Elise smiled even through the sheen of tears. "Thank you for your son."

They walked together, both wiping away tears. It had been a long road, but the gift of forgiveness was never given without receiving something in return. For the first time in years Elise was completely at peace. Life still had its troubles, but God continued to flood her with His strength every single day.

Elise wiped away tears. Today wasn't a day for sadness, it was a day for healing.

A day to embrace the future.

As she walked toward Jonah, she felt her lips curl up in a smile. She had planned to wait until their quiet dinner date to tell him her news, but didn't think she'd be able to now. It was still very early, but they had both waited years for this life.

She wasn't wasting a single minute of it.

Jonah smiled as she walked toward him. Even though she'd been crying, she was still the most beautiful woman he'd ever seen. Elise had suffered her share of hard times, but hadn't let life bring her down. Now she was imparting that to him every single day, showing him how to embrace a full life, and how to be a husband and father.

While his mom and Nathan got into the car, Jonah pulled Elise into his arms. "Okay?"

She smiled up at him and nodded. "I am. I'm better than okay, because I have you."

Every time she said it, his heart swelled with love.

"And our child will have both of us, for his or her whole life."

Jonah tried to inhale, but it got stuck. "Our... Seriously?"

She nodded.

"Elise." She couldn't be serious, could she?

"Yes, Jonah?"

"We're having a baby?"

She nodded, placing her hands on his cheeks. "We're having a baby."

Jonah lifted her, spinning her around until she squealed and he set her back on her feet. "Oops. Sorry."

But she was grinning. Jonah felt like his cheeks were going to split, he was smiling so wide.

"Thank you."

She smiled wider. "You're very welcome, Jonah."

Jonah had everything he'd always dreamed of. And while he knew life wasn't always going to be perfect, whatever happened, they would face it together.

* * * * *

Dear Reader,

Thank you for going through this journey with me. Elise and Jonah had the blessing of a rich friendship behind them, but misguided choices and time held them apart. Elise grieved the loss of her husband, but had his son's presence in her life to give her hope.

God will often give us blessings at the same time He holds back what we "think" we need. I've found this to be true in my life. I'll be praying for you, dear reader, in whatever season of life you're in. God will always prove Himself faithful if we trust Him to work all things for good in our lives.

To find out more about my books, you can go to authorlisaphillips.com or you can always email me at lisaphillipsbks@gmail.com. If you're not online, you can write to me c/o Love Inspired Books, 233 Broadway, Suite 1001, New York, NY 10279.

I would love to hear from you.

God richly bless you,
Lisa Phillips